The Vampire
and the Case of Her
Dastardly Death

Heather G. Harris & Jilleen Dolbeare

Published by Hellhound Press Limited

HELLHOUND
PRESS

Foreword

If you'd like to hear the latest gossip, bargains and new releases from us, then please join our newsletters!

If you'd like FREE BOOKS then join Heather's newsletter and you can get a couple of free stories, as well as pictures of her dog and other helpful things.

Jill will also give you FREE BOOKS, but she will send you cat images instead! Sign up to Jill's Newsletter here.

Dedication

Heather's dedication:

Thanks to my awesome supporters on Patreon, with special mention to Amanda Peterman, Melissa and Kassandra.

Thanks to my husband, for his unending patience, to Beba for her endless cheerleading, and finally to Jill. Thanks Jill for agreeing to play with me. Planning this series together has been a hilarious mix of late night conversations, google docs, and memes that have made us laugh together, and I'm grateful for every moment of it. It has been an absolute blast, long may it continue.

Jilleen's dedication:

First off, thanks to Heather. She and I published our first books at the same time. She reached out to me to ask if I'd do a newsletter swap with her. I said, 'What's that?' and she's been there for me ever since, showing me how it's done. She's an inspiration, a great mum, a lovely friend, a brilliant writer, and best of all, a wonderful human.

Content Warnings

Please see the full content warnings on Heather's website if you are concerned about triggers.

The *Portlock Paranormal Detective* series has scenes of violence and poor language is occasionally used.

Please note that all of Heather's works are written in *British English* with British phrases, spellings and grammar being utilised throughout.

Jilleen has gamely joined her in adopting British English but she is American. If any Americanisms slip though the net, or if you think you have found a typo, please do let Heather know at heathergharrisauthor@gmail.com. Thank you!

Chapter 1

I woke up dead. I just didn't know it.

I lurched upright, feeling sore and weird. I'd had the oddest dream that I'd been attacked by a vampire. I touched my neck instinctively – and froze at the wince of pain. Oh no. Hell, no. I stumbled into the bathroom and that's when I noticed that my heart wasn't beating.

My heart wasn't beating? Fuck.

I flipped on the bathroom light and shrieked. I had dried blood all around my mouth, and my normally pale skin was even paler, almost translucent. My hair was a tangled mess, and my emerald-green eyes were brighter, though bloodshot. I reluctantly bared my teeth and gave a little yelp at the sight of protruding fangs.

Oh my God. It wasn't a dream.

What had happened at the club last night? I thought back. I'd been snogging Franklin in the back corner and the bastard had bitten me! It all came flooding back: he'd bitten me and then I'd drunk his blood. A lot of blood. Yuck! What was I thinking? Of course, I'd had several Jager shots by that point plus a few cocktails, a couple of tequila shots, and something blue...

My heart thudded, just once, but it was enough to make me sag with relief – I still had a heartbeat. A lethargic one, but still. Better than no heartbeat at all. Maybe I wasn't human any more, but I was still human-adjacent, right? I still had a reflection according to the mirror I was staring at.

I wanted to panic but it wasn't happening, maybe because my heart couldn't beat fast enough. Maybe I needed time for this disaster to hit me. That had to be it: I was in denial land. I'd been practising denial for most of my life, and I could do it all day long. And it wasn't like vampires were a complete shock to me; I knew they existed.

I took a deep breath and my fangs retracted, leaving me with normal-looking teeth. Cool; my teeth had an incognito mode.

I knew very little about vampires. I'd studiously ignored my dad's shady business partner, as much as one could ignore the vampire king of Europe, but I knew they were real. And now I was one. Man, Mum was going to kill me. Again.

The gallows humour made me smile bleakly. Okay, I could do this. How bad could eternal night be?

There was a polite rap at the door. 'Elizabeth,' my mother called, exasperated. 'Open this pathetic excuse for a door.'

Mum has the worst timing. I ignored her, hoping she'd go away, but the polite knocking continued. If she saw me like this, *she'd* probably die and I'd be responsible for my prissy mother having a heart attack. I couldn't cope with the thought of that; although we rarely get on, I couldn't lose her – not so soon after Nana.

I looked cautiously in the mirror again but my appearance was unchanged. My mascara was streaking my cheeks, and my chin and neck were still smeared with blood. I wet the flannel and started to scrub frantically at myself. 'Just a minute, Mum,' I called reluctantly.

'Elizabeth Octavia Barrington, open this door right now!' she commanded imperiously. 'Before the neighbours see me,' she muttered.

That certainly wouldn't do. My mother hates being spotted in places that don't fit her idea of posh, and my studio apartment was not on the list. It wasn't anywhere near the list; it wasn't even on the same page. Frankly, I was surprised she even knew where I lived.

She wasn't going to go away, so now I was going to have to open the door and face the music. Even if the music was screaming death metal.

Chapter 2

I hastily finished cleaning up, brushed my long ash-blonde hair and pulled it back into a ponytail. I zipped up my jacket to hide the two small puncture wounds still visible on my neck and opened the door.

I hope she wouldn't notice how pale I was. Blood loss does that to a girl. 'Hi, Mum.'

She pushed me aside and walked in, scanning the room and scowling at the old, mismatched furniture. My flat smelled faintly like the Chinese restaurant next door, and her lips pinched further. She glared at the sofa with a wrinkle to her nose then brushed it clean before sitting primly on the edge of it.

I'd put on my slippers so I hoped she'd think that I was wearing my pyjamas, but actually I was still in my clubbing clothes from the night before. I hoped my leather jacket covered most of them; Mother would disapprove of the low-necked, tight-fitting dress. Plus it was black, and she loathes me wearing black.

I'd just had the worst night of my life, which apparently had included my death. The reason I'd gone out was because I'd already had the worst *day* of my life. I wasn't ready for the lecture though I knew it was coming – it always did.

I raised my eyebrows, waiting for her to tell me the reason she'd come by at seven in the morning. Even though it was dreadfully early for her – or dreadfully late for me, perspective and all that – she was impeccably groomed. Her hair, artfully dyed the same ash blonde as my own, was perfectly sculpted. Her makeup looked like she kept a professional on call and her emerald-green eyes, the twins of mine, were bright and awake. She was wearing a boring, if expensive, baby blue dress. The only thing that marred her perfection was her frown at the disarray in my flat. Lines were etched on her forehead, though I knew that if I mentioned them they'd be gone in an instant.

My flat... I grimaced. Discarded clothes lay strewn about, left over from my rush to get ready the previous night, and there was a sink full of dirty dishes. I still hadn't gotten around to fitting curtains or blinds in the kitchen area either. To call the flat "rough and ready" was probably being overgenerous, but it was all I could afford on my shitty salary since my parents had cut me off. Apparently, they wanted me to "stand on my own two feet", which was fine in theory but I'd been toddling on stilts ever since. I fell over frequently and skinned my knees, but I'd been doing it. Until I'd gotten killed, anyway.

Mum returned her focus to me and cleared her throat. 'I'm here to remind you to have an acceptable date for the wedding next weekend.'

I blinked. She'd braved my flat for that? 'You could have phoned,' I pointed out drily.

'Yes, but I wanted to see you, Elizabeth. You didn't come by yesterday even though you said you would.'

Crap, I *had* said that I would visit, but getting fired had totally railroaded my plans. Ugh ... guilt: the currency of mothers everywhere.

I hadn't gone because I couldn't face telling her that I'd lost yet another deadbeat job. It wasn't as if my upbringing had prepared me to wait tables; you'd think with an eidetic memory I could have found something more suitable. But no; most potential employers thought it weird that I could recall the exact words spoken to me fifteen years ago when I was eight years old.

The worst thing was that I hadn't even wanted to go out last night but my friends had wanted to make me feel better. Instead, they'd got me killed.

I looked away. Mum is like a bloodhound: she'd sniff out my problems and be all over me like white on rice, just like always. The most I could hope for was to delay her judgement, which I knew I'd get in spades.

No one ever tells you that being an only child brings its own problems. I was a disappointment to her – and now that I was a vampire, I could be an *eternal* disappointment to her. God, I'd live forever unless I got staked one day. I saw my mother's judgemental gaze and thought that getting staked would be something to look forward to.

'Sorry, Mum. I was busy,' I offered lamely.

'Were you working?'

I looked away; I had been working until the *incident*. 'Yes.' I must have added a tiny inflection at the end because she pounced.

She raised her thin, perfectly waxed eyebrow. 'What happened, Elizabeth?'

I stood up with a sigh. I couldn't keep anything from her so there was no point trying. Besides, being fired wasn't going to feel like a big deal when I told her I'd accidentally joined the hidden army of the bitey undead. 'I was fired,' I said brusquely.

'Again?' she asked coolly.

I sat down again and slumped against the soft, worn cushions.

Her lips pressed together. 'Sit up straight, dear. Posture is important.'

I sat up automatically; I'd heard those words a thousand times. But why would I give a fuck about posture when my heart was only beating five measly times a minute?

'What was the reason this time?' Mum's tone indicated that she absolutely believed that *I* was to blame.

'I was serving a table with several men. They thought my name implied a willingness to be fondled, so I dumped the tray of drinks on them.'

Her mouth twisted in a moue of distaste. 'I'll never understand why you insist on going by that name.'

'Bunny is my name, Mum. It fits me,' I argued for the millionth time.

'Your name is Elizabeth,' she grouched.

The age-old argument grated on me. I'd gone by the name Bunny for more years than by the name she'd foisted on me. 'No, Elizabeth is the name *you* gave me, but it was never *me*.'

'I refuse to call you Bunny.'

I shrugged. As usual, she'd missed the whole point. 'Anyway, one man grabbed my bum and somehow, when I retaliated, the manager took his side and fired me on the spot.'

'What did you expect, dear? You are in a service industry. You can't dump drinks on paying customers.'

'I expect not to be groped at work,' I groused, arms folded.

'Yes of course, but you should have handled it differently.'

Sure I *could* have, but that wasn't the point. I was without a job again. My temper and lack of actual work skills were once again leaving me jobless and, without an income, probably homeless.

Not to mention, a new and far more pressing issue. If vampires were allergic to sunlight like the tales said, then I couldn't afford to be homeless. I'd have to move back in with my *parents.*

I wished I knew more about vampires, but my parents had always insisted that I stayed far away from all the meetings that went on behind doors, and truthfully I'd been more than willing to indulge them. Who wanted to learn about creepy blood-drinking creatures? I'd been happy to pretend that vampires were nothing more than a bedtime story.

Ugh. Who had I screwed over in a previous life to deserve this fresh hell? I looked away, feeling hot tears well up.

'What in God's name is *that*?' My mother's voice was sharp.

Oh fuck.

Chapter 3

I whipped my head back. 'What's what?' I asked innocently, eyes wide.

'Those marks on your neck, are they ... love bites?' she asked, horrified. The truth was going to horrify her even more.

My hand leapt up to my throat to cover the telltale pricks in my neck.

'No!' She reached out to pull my hand and the jacket collar away, displaying the bite in all its vampiric glory. 'Is that...?' Her voice trailed away, shocked and dismayed. She shook her head. 'No, that's silly. They wouldn't dare...'

I could see the fear in her eyes. There was no point trying to hide what had happened. Her long association with Dad's business meant that she knew what the marks were as surely as I did, for all she was practising denial right now – it wasn't just a river in Egypt.

I decided to say it quickly, like ripping off a plaster. 'I've been bitten, Mum. It looks like I'm a vampire.'

She clutched her pearls and sat down heavily on the sofa. 'What have you done now?' she whispered, shaking her head. 'What will I tell the Winthrop-Smythes? We'll be social outcasts.'

I groaned. Of course, that would be her take away. I was dead, our family line would die with me, and all she cared about was what the bloody Winthrop-Smythes would think!

'It wasn't my fault,' I said tightly, pointing at my throat. The tears were back – and so were my fangs. I touched them with my tongue. Great. How was I going to do this, navigate this, alone? I didn't know how to be a vampire. It wasn't like the bite had come with an owner's manual.

Mum frowned and sighed heavily. 'Of course it wasn't. I suppose the Winthrop-Smythes don't need to know everything. We can keep this quiet. We'll tell everyone at the wedding that you've developed a skin condition that means you're allergic to light. We can salvage this.'

She was already plotting. My life was ruined, and she was still worried about the bloody wedding. I wiped away a tear that was trickling down my face. 'I...'

There was a sharp knock at the door. Mum leapt up and looked around for somewhere to hide. She wouldn't be seen dead here, but unless she wanted to jump into my tiny bathroom and crouch on the loo there wasn't anywhere for her to go.

'I doubt anyone you know will be at my door,' I reassured her as I walked the three steps to it and opened the flimsy plywood structure.

As well as a brilliant memory, I am also excellent at deductive reasoning. On the other side of my door stood a bike messenger; I knew that from the bike helmet on his head and the bike he'd carried up the three flights of winding stairs. See? I was just like Sherlock Holmes, but female and a vampire. Great.

He thrust a large envelope at me and waited a beat to see if he'd get a tip. Yeah, that was a no. My ass was fired and I couldn't even spare a pound. I gave him a bright smile instead, but he recoiled at the sight of my fangs. Oh shit. Note to self: closed-mouth smiles from here on in until I got those things under control.

My mum was on it, though. She leapt forward and thrust a ten-pound note at him, hoping to distract him from my fangy *faux pas*. He faked tipping his helmet at her and left quickly, giving me a backwards glance as he all but ran away.

I stared down at my name written in a neat, flowing script, the finest calligraphy. No one I knew wrote like that, not these days. I'd learned early on that I didn't like events that came with an inscribed invitation; I prefer the ones that come by text. I turned the envelope over a couple of times to see who it was from, but there was nothing else on it.

'Well, open it, dear,' my mother instructed impatiently.

For some reason, I was terrified about opening it, as if a previously unknown sense of self-preservation had shown up twenty-three years late and was warning me.

The instinctual feeling could go to hell. Where had it been last night when I'd needed it? I blew out a harsh breath. I hated doing what my mother told me to do, but it looked like I'm going to have to open the damned envelope.

Chapter 4

I swallowed, my mouth salivating, making me gulp compulsively as if I were on the verge of vomiting. The envelope had a red wax seal and I recognised the insignia – I'd seen it before. On an envelope strewn across Dad's desk on the one occasion I'd snuck into his office. That was how I'd found out vampires were real, and my father was embroiled hip deep in their business. After that, Dad had made sure I never found my way into his office ever again, but the damage was done. I'd read the vampire king's letter.

Looking at the envelope in my hand, I had the opposite urge. I knew without a doubt that I didn't want to open it, but I also knew that ignoring the vampire king was probably a sure-fire way to get permanently dead. I slid a nail under the red wax, and it popped satisfyingly. Inside was a single sheet of luxurious paper.

I scanned it hurriedly, wanting to be done with it. My hand started to shake. Mum watched me with trepidation. She was dying to know what it said. I was summoned to an audience with the king. The phraseology didn't make it seem like my attendance was optional. I turned it over. The address to attend was on the back. When I was done staring at the invite blankly, I held it out to Mum. She snatched it from me and started reading.

'The vampire king!' she shrieked. 'Who the hell bit you?'

I looked away, ashamed I'd been sucked into this whole sordid affair – pun intended. If my murky dreams were right, I knew who had done the dastardly deed; after all, I'd spent half the night playing tonsil hockey with him. Only being severely impaired by booze had made that seem like a good idea. I was *never* drinking again.

'His son,' I admitted reluctantly. That particular decision would forever be the top of my list of mistakes. No matter how long I lived, it was always going to be at the top, emblazoned in neon lights. Why had I approached *him*? I knew full well what he was. I'd seen him come to the house to meet with Dad in his father's stead.

Dramatic as always, my mother let the paper drift to the ground and clutched a hand to her chest. At least *she* still had a decent heartbeat. 'Which son?'

Magic and the supernatural world may be unknown to the world at large, but my family had apparently been dealing with the vampires since my dad started his company. The vampires are still very much in the closet; people know about them as a folklore tale, but if you say you think they're real, people think you're a few cards short of a full deck.

My family knows better. *I* should have known better. Even worse, the son that had bitten me was the worst, and I'd always avoided him when he'd come to my parents' house. I had no idea what foolishness had come over me to make me prance up to him last night. *Bad decision, Bunny.*

'Franklin,' I admitted.

Mum's hand fluttered to her forehead in a typical 'you'll be the death of me' gesture. What could I say? My actions had already been the death of me.

'It's not like I planned it – I didn't ask for any of this.' I could feel a band tightening around my chest as I fought back the tears and panic.

I didn't know what to do. If I appeared before the king, as he'd demanded, what would happen to me? In the one conversation I'd had with my dad about the vampires, he'd totally freaked out. He told me that vampires were tightly controlled and their king wasn't a nice figurehead like ours. He was a tyrant, a despot, a dictator.

I supposed he was now my king, too. What a goddamn mess. I clutched my arms around my middle to hold myself together. I couldn't deal with this right now. I needed a distraction, something to keep my mother from seeing my tears.

As I looked desperately around, my eyes settled on the dirty dishes. Now was the perfect time for a spot of cleaning. I turned on the hot water, watched the sink fill up and then reached across to pull some dirty dishes into the suds. As I did so, my hand passed through a beam of early-morning sun. It felt like a laser had burned me.

I yelped and yanked back my arm with a curse. The skin bubbled up, red, raw and blistered. I looked at the weak sunbeam streaming in and winced. Right: vampire, no sunlight. At least there weren't any more windows in my tiny flat, just this pathetic one.

As I stumbled backwards, reality hit me like a truck. 'I d-d-don't knoooow how to do this-s-s,' I cried. A desperate sob escaped me. I was exhausted, hurt and utterly lost.

'Oh, darling. Let's see.' Mum grabbed my arm and looked at it.

To my relief, it was already healing, although the burn continued to ache. 'Why is the burn healing and not my bite marks?' I sniffled.

'The marks from your sire will never fade. They'll close over in a few days, but eventually they'll scar. Other injuries will heal before you can say Bob's your uncle, but that doesn't mean they won't hurt.' How did she know so much about vampires? Perhaps she hadn't been willing to be woefully ignorant, like me. To say that felt like a mistake now was a gross understatement. I should have dug into it, no matter what Dad had said.

Mum looked around then grabbed the throw from the back of the sofa and flung it over the curtain rod at the window. It didn't look pretty, but it would do the job. I was suddenly very grateful for the lack of sunlight.

I closed my eyes and pushed back the tears and despair. Now wasn't the time to panic. I needed to rest; something in my body was saying that daylight wasn't my friend, and sleep was calling to me like a siren. 'I'm tired, Mum. I'm going to bed.'

'Of course, darling.' She looked a little lost as well, but she is very practised at the British stiff upper lip. She nodded, kissed me on the cheek and left.

Exhaustion clawed at me and I fell down on the bed. Before I drifted off to sleep – or death – I had one thought: when would I crave blood?

Chapter 5

I awoke to a rude pounding on the door: bang, bang, bang. My cheap, flimsy door wasn't so strong that it could withstand much of that, so I leapt up hastily to open it.

When I cracked it open cautiously, no one was there. I looked down the hallway towards the creaky stairs but no one was visible. I glanced down and saw a package. I hadn't ordered anything; I had no money for anything beyond the necessities like food. Small things like that.

I double-checked the label: it was written out to Elizabeth O. Barrington with my address scrawled on it. I shrugged and picked up the box; it wasn't particularly large but it was surprisingly heavy. What was even more surprising was how easy it was for me to lift despite its weight. So there *were* upsides to being a vampire. Maybe it wouldn't be so bad after all. That's better, all I needed was some optimism.

I placed the box on the kitchen counter and looked for a knife to slice through the tape. I grabbed a kitchen knife and then hesitated. The last twenty-four hours had taught me that I should exercise caution. The box was cardboard, brand new, and some of the corners looked sharp. This hadn't been sent by one of my friends; they re-used boxes to help the environment and besides, they would have addressed a package to Bunny. I set the knife down, biting my lip.

I wondered for a ridiculous moment if the box would go boom. Mum had always taught me to be wary of unidentified objects; she'd taken her talks about Stranger Danger to a whole new level. Feeling ridiculous, I pressed my ear to the box and listened to it. There was no ticking – bombs tick, right?

I grabbed the knife again; I was being silly. Even if anyone beyond my family and the vampires already knew about my sudden bout of vampirism – which was doubtful because Mum would die before she admitted my latest shame – I wasn't worth the effort or expense of a big kaboom. I doubt failed waitresses were often targeted for assassination.

With that happy thought, I sliced the tape and opened the box. It was insulated, with a typed packing slip on top. Inside were numerous bags of blood of various types.

I felt my stomach lurch. Oh hell. Dinner had been served. Under the packing slip was a list of instructions, including portion-size recommendations, heating instructions and storage requirements. Yikes: who knew a blood diet would be so particular?

Although I emptied the box, I couldn't find out who it was from. The options were slim – either my mother had sent it, or the vamps. I opened my small refrigerator and looked at its contents: a bottle of sparkling water, a limp spring onion and a small jar of yellow mustard. I grimaced. At least there was plenty of space for the blood bags.

My stomach rumbled. I had a single slice of bread left and, without thinking, I popped it in the toaster.

Apart from the mustard I didn't have anything to put on it, but dry toast was still better than blood. *Anything* was better than blood. I felt no urge to drink the stuff, let alone drain anyone dry. If it wasn't for the package full of bags of blood, I'd be doubting whether vampires really did subsist on the stuff.

The second the toast popped up, I shoved it into my mouth like I hadn't eaten for a year. I was starving and my guts felt like they were gnawing me alive. The toast barely touched my hunger so I looked around for something else. Short of the wilted spring onion, there was nothing.

I peeked cautiously around the makeshift curtain. Night had fallen, thank goodness, so I could run to the corner shop. I found my bag and searched through it to see if I had any tips left from my former job, but I scrounged without luck. I'd used all my cash at the club last night. I grimaced; last-night-Bunny had been making bad choices.

I had just over a hundred pounds in the bank, but I'd need that to survive until I found a new job. At least my rent was paid a month in advance. I searched all my clothes and the cushions in the sofa and pulled together almost five pounds, enough for a sandwich at least.

I sniffed my jeans; they'd do. I pulled them on, together with a comparatively clean T-shirt, and shoved my jacket back on. I was ready for the quick trip to the shops. I didn't have much cash but I needed *something* to help me face the vampire court without passing out. I couldn't face the blood bags in my fridge. Not yet.

Just before I ran out of the door, a tearing pain came from my guts. It was so bad that I barely made it into the bathroom before my measly piece of toast started reappearing. Luckily, I got there in time to worship the porcelain bowl. Ugh: I hate being sick.

Okay, so no toast. I didn't even know if vampires could eat regular food. I cast my mind back. Franklin and his cohorts from last night had been drinking something for sure, but I suppose it could have been blood held in the bar's coloured glasses.

I cleaned myself up as my guts went back to their gnawing hunger. Reluctantly, I opened the fridge door again. Was blood my only choice? I hated being told what to do, even if it were something as simple as what I could eat.

The blood bags stared at me, taunting me. My stomach gave an audible growl. Damn it.

'Come on, Bunny,' I said to myself. 'Don't be such a baby. You're a vampire now.' The problem was, I didn't feel like a vampire; I just felt like me, only more scared of sunlight.

I took out a bag. It was O neg, the universal donor. Lucky me. I scoured the box for the instructions then measured out one mug full, the recommended serving size for my weight. It seemed a pitiful amount. More like the amount you'd feed a pet cat. I shook my head then I stuck the cup in the microwave for the prescribed twenty seconds.

When it was warm, I looked at it dubiously. I gave it a little sniff; it didn't smell *that* bad, more like a meaty broth. My stomach rumbled loudly. At least *it* was excited about the prospect of food. I closed my eyes so I didn't have to see the colour then pinched my nostrils and swigged it, glugging it down as quickly as

I could manage. Suddenly I was grateful for the many beer-chugging contests I'd taken part in at university.

I hurriedly rinsed my cup, the better to wash away the bloody evidence that I definitely wasn't normal any more. My stomach was thankfully still and finally happy. I felt comfortably full and the gnawing had stopped. I put the rest of the blood bag back in the fridge. The aftertaste in my mouth was surprisingly pleasant. As much as I hated the idea, it had been edible. Drinkable? I shrugged. Palatable.

Now full, at least I didn't need to spend my paltry five pounds. I could save it for tomorrow's food. That was a relief, but it brought another thought. Would I even have to eat other foods? I am a foodie and honestly, a diet of blood three times a day forever sounded incredibly dull. What about ice cream? Did vamps eat ice cream? Maybe it had to be blood ice cream? I shuddered.

I knew that I should probably be writing down questions because it turned out that I knew next to nothing about vampires. I railed against my wilful ignorance now that my survival depended on learning everything about vampires. I checked the time; I didn't have time to write down questions. In fact, I'd have to hurry if I was to make my royal summons. Shit.

Chapter 6

I looked down at my current outfit. I couldn't wear slightly dirty jeans to meet a king. I sniffed myself and recoiled. All of my panic at meeting the king had induced quite the sweat. My sense of smell was better than ever and I was now a little pungent. I peeled off my clothes, hastily went into the bathroom and had a speed shower before drying myself and my hair.

Clean and dry, I searched for something to wear. What did one wear to see a king? I had club clothes and work clothes, but jeans were probably out, as were miniskirts. I searched through my tiny wardrobe. It was packed tight since I had a lot of clothes from before I'd moved out of my parent's house. Nice things, if boring. I brightened: nice and boring was probably exactly what the vampire king ordered.

I pulled out a navy dress with large white polka dots. It had a tie in the middle and a white collar, was knee length and *extremely* conservative. Definitely something my mother had bought for me. I checked: yup, the tags were still on it. Expensive, silk, and completely *not* me. I pulled it on. Not me sounded good right now.

I threw my hair up in a messy chignon, leaving wispy curls to frame my face. I painted on some lipstick and a swipe of mascara. I added little kitten heels to the mix, completing the perfectly boring outfit. Mum would be proud.

I took a deep breath, smoothed the dress and walked out the door. It was time to meet a king.

I looked dubiously at the address on the card then back up at the gargantuan tower block in front of me: twenty-one floors, including what looked like a rooftop terrace. I'd expected a palace or a castle, not an office building.

Two men in dark suits and sunglasses were standing outside the entrance. They looked like they thought they were badass, but the sunglasses made me laugh. Who wore sunglasses in the dead of night? Tough guys, apparently. No doubt they were highly trained vampire operatives or something.

I marched towards them, giving them my friendliest smile but neither of them acknowledged me. Not knowing what else to do, I gave a little finger wave but they still didn't respond. Rude.

The one on the right was rocking slightly on his heels, rubbing together his right forefinger and thumb. Even in the poor light I could see the stain of yellow on his fingers. He was jonesing for a cigarette and for some reason that reassured me. Vampires still had human flaws.

The doorman was dressed in a suit and top hat. It was overkill, but I supposed that was the vampire king's MO. He opened the door for me and I thanked him politely; being undead was no excuse for rudeness.

Once I was inside, I wasn't sure what to do. I went up to the reception desk and told the woman there that I had an appointment. I didn't mention the V word because there was a chance she was a normal human – it was unlikely, but it was still possible.

The receptionist gave me a cool look and, gesturing towards an uncomfortable looking wooden bench, told me to take a seat. It reminded me of an old-fashioned pew in a church. I sat down. It had taken sixteen paces to get to the benches; I had counted them reflexively. I always notice weird things.

I resisted the urge to hum or twiddle my thumbs. I was the only one waiting in the cavernous entry hall and my anxiety led to boredom pretty quickly. The whole place was eerily quiet. Beyond me, over what seemed like acres of marble, was a bank of lifts. Six lifts, four doors, one exit, one fire exit. I studied the receptionist instead, noting her long painted nails and the plethora of rings on her fingers. Thirteen rings seemed like too many for someone with ten fingers.

I waited for what felt like forever. Eventually, I heard the faintest scuff of shoes, and looked up to see a man approaching. I had no idea where he'd come from, unless he'd used a lift; if so, it had been utterly silent. He was wearing a dark suit; his leather shoes abnormally quiet except for that one scuffling sound.

The hair on my neck stood up uneasily. The man before me was a predator.

He finally spoke. 'Ms Barrington?'

'Yes.' I nodded decisively, trying to bury my nerves.

'Follow me.' He turned and walked towards the lifts. Fear burned in my gut and I hoped to hell he couldn't sense it. Predators loved that sort of thing, right?

I gave myself a quick pep talk, stood and followed him for my appointment with the king of death.

Chapter 7

Once we were inside the lift, the thickset man waved a card in front of a reader and punched in the top floor, the rooftop terrace. That was either brave or foolhardy; it was night just now but a vampire having a meeting on the roof showed serious balls or a lack of a good frontal lobe.

I leaned against the back wall of the lift. Although we went up twenty-one floors, it was quiet, fast and I hardly felt the movement. I was taken aback when the doors pinged open.

I hadn't been sure what to expect. What did a vampire court look like? This whole building had posh-office vibes so I'd thought maybe rattan furniture, glass tables and small potted trees on the terrace. Instead the space was completely open and barren. Marble flooring continued onto the roof, endless and gleaming white.

In the centre of the space was an honest-to-goodness throne; there was no other word to describe it. The luxurious wooden chair was gilded, edged in ermine and had sumptuous purple-brocade cushions. The throne had an occupant and flanking it was a posse of other vampires. No one spoke; all eyes were on me. Lucky me.

The man guiding me cleared his throat and I realised he was trying to get me to step out of the lift instead of staring out of it like an idiot. 'Sorry,' I mumbled and stepped out.

The hulking henchman escorted me to the throne, a hand in the small of my back propelling me forwards. Clearly, he didn't trust me to get there under my own steam. He wasn't wrong to assume that. My legs were stiff with fear.

The vampire king wasn't that exciting to look at: medium height, medium build, and nondescript in a you-wouldn't-look-at-him-twice kind of way. Then you met his eyes – and they were anything but ordinary. They burned with intelligence and power.

I desperately wanted to look away, but I forced myself to meet them. This was the *top* predator and if I fled, I was afraid he'd chase me, so I held his gaze out of sheer stubbornness.

My guide bowed before his king and went back to stand in front of the lift, a silent sentinel. The king's two sons and their bodyguards stood on either side of him. One of the vampires was holding a book. Three other men stood behind them, probably the king's bodyguards, although from what little I knew of my dad's business partner I expect he took care of all threats himself.

I wasn't sure what to do so I curtsied briefly and waited. The silence was taut and uncomfortable. I wanted to wriggle and fidget but I forced myself to stay still. I knew nothing about vampire law, and I didn't want to cause offence by accident – when I cause offence, I want it to be on purpose. Still, the strained silence stretched. Vampires have all the time in the world, I supposed. They can go around having ridiculous pauses if they want. The absurdity of it did make me relax a fraction, though I expect the silence was designed to have the opposite effect.

The king broke the silence, 'Elizabeth Octavia Barrington, I presume?' The king's voice was a deep bass that rumbled out of his chest.

I hate that bloody name. 'Bunny is fine,' I said.

He raised an eyebrow. 'A vampire named Bunny?' He gave a sharp laugh. The laugh took away the sinister air and I relaxed a fraction further. 'How did you get that nickname?' he asked curiously.

I'd heard this question a million times and I trotted out one of my favourite answers. 'A teacher at school gave it to me when I was five after I spent a week hopping for no apparent reason,' I lied baldly.

'And you kept it?' He laughed again.

I felt my face trying to flush, though presumably that was difficult now with my sluggish heart. Bunny fits me so much better than 'Elizabeth Octavia', which is nothing but pretentious and uppity.

'It's my name,' I said simply. Social climbing is in my mother's makeup, not mine, hence her naming me Elizabeth Octavia. Bunny is happy, light, fun, and that's what I wanted to be.

'Well, Bunny, I must apologize for my son.' He threw a dark look at Franklin, who was staring sulkily at me.

Franklin's jaw tightened in anger as he met my gaze. I was making friends everywhere.

'Since he turned you against your will and did not follow the strict turning protocol, we will give you seven days to get your affairs in order before you join the conclave.'

Conclave? What conclave? My breath caught and I looked around for an answer, any answer. 'I'm sorry, Your...' Did I call him Your Majesty? Sir? What? 'Umm, Majesty. What is the conclave?'

He blinked; I'd obviously surprised him. 'Didn't your parents speak of us at all?'

'No,' I admitted.

'Vampires must live under the control of the court until they have served for one hundred years. At that time, they may petition to be released if they have shown control and are not a danger to the public.'

He smiled but there was no humour in it. 'We can't afford media scrutiny these days. Normally you would enter the conclave straight away but in recognition of your ... situation ... you have a week to get your affairs in order. Until your seven days are up, Franklin will stay with you to keep you safe and ensure you are not a danger to others.'

The noise from Franklin seemed to be a protest, but the king talked over it. 'I suggest you give notice at your job and pack up your things. After we review your skills, we'll put you in an entry-level job that suits your skillset.'

I didn't interrupt to tell him I had no job nor skillset.

'We will supply you with blood until you receive your first pay cheque, at which point you will be expected to pay for it.'

I frowned. 'I don't have a choice in this?'

'My word is absolute.' He waved at one of the suits who stepped forward and handed me a book.

I glanced down. *How to Survive Your First One Hundred Years as a Vampire*. Shit. The bite *did* come with a manual. 'I don't...' But before I could finish my statement...

'Dismissed.'

The hulking henchman grabbed my elbow and steered me back to the lifts. I guessed my audience was over, as well as my life. Franklin had better steer clear of me because I would be kicking him in the bollocks the minute he was close enough.

Chapter 8

I was furious as I clutched the book and walked briskly down the still-dark street to the tube station. I checked the time on my phone: early morning. Hopefully, I'd be home before sunrise. Otherwise, I'd be barbeque.

I clenched my teeth so hard that I felt a sharp bite as my fangs descended and bit into the inside of my cheek. Ouch! I spat blood onto the well-lit sidewalk. A woman stopped to check on me, but she took one look at my rage-filled face and rapidly backed away.

I looked around. Yup: several people were staring. 'My boyfriend beats me,' I lied. Domestic violence makes people feel awkward. Sure enough, they turned away.

I had a couple of blood spots on my silk dress. The ones on the navy weren't too visible but the ones on the white polka dots stood out a mile. Never mind, the dress was going straight in the bin anyway. It had bad associations now and besides, getting blood out of silk is tedious. Plus, I hated the dress.

I walked fast. What was I going to do? I had to live under the thumb of a monster for a hundred years? I couldn't do that – I'd left home so I could be free. I was breathing hard; I had to slow down, or I'd hyperventilate.

I stopped in the street and started to try to regulate my breathing. 'Bunny!' a man yelled at me. I turned to see Franklin running after me. Just great. That absolute bastard. 'Wait up!'

Nope. Not a chance. I started to walk faster to get away from him. Then I heard someone yell, 'Get him!'

I whirled around. Two men had stopped Franklin and one was punching him in the stomach. I wanted to laugh but it didn't seem wise.

'We'll help you, honey,' a woman said next to me. 'Your boyfriend won't hurt you again. The police are on their way.'

Shit. That wouldn't go down well with the king. Much as I wanted Franklin to get what was coming to him, I'd have to intervene. I didn't want to lose my last seven days of freedom. I thought quickly. 'Oh no!' I said. 'That's not my boyfriend, that's my, uh, brother.'

The woman gave me a look that said she didn't buy it for a minute, and her eyes were sorrowful as I went to save what she thought was my abuser. She wasn't actually wrong in that supposition.

I hurried over to where the men were still whaling on him. 'Stop, that's my brother!' I entreated.

'Brother?' The men stopped and let go of Franklin.

'Yes, he was coming to help me. Thank you for stepping in. If he'd been my boyfriend, I'd have been really grateful!'

'Sorry, miss. Our mistake,' one of the men said.

'Sorry, mate.' The other one brushed Franklin off and they both walked hurriedly away.

Sirens were approaching. 'Get in the car,' Franklin growled.

I looked over. There was a black Mercedes idling at the curb. 'I'm fine. I'll take the tube.' I turned to leave.

He grabbed my arm and yanked me over to the car. I whirled on him but at the last second, he let me go; he obviously didn't think I was a threat. Huh. I'd show him – I'd promised myself, after all.

I kneed him squarely in the bollocks. 'That's for killing me ... "accidentally".' I put up air quotes and let my sarcasm hang in the air. There was no way he'd turned me by accident, no matter what line he'd fed to his father.

When he'd killed me by drinking too much of my blood – without my permission, I might add, he'd desperately fed me his own blood to save his lousy hide. I was hazy from blood loss while he did it, but from what I remembered he'd said, 'Shit, too much.'

That memory just fuelled my rage so I kneed him again. 'And that's for being an utter twat.' It seemed even vampires couldn't take the pain of a knee to the jewels. Franklin doubled over and fell to the pavement, clutching his junk.

I walked the last street to the tube and jogged down the stairs to the platform. Luckily, the train came within a minute. I hopped on and watched with relief as the doors slid shut. I was sure I'd pay for my action, but the momentary satisfaction would hopefully see me through the next seven days.

The tube ride was short, and I hastily made tracks to my flat. No doubt the king and his cohorts had my address, but they weren't there yet, so I had some temporary respite.

I opened my door and looked around at my home in despair. It wouldn't take me seven days to pack; it would take me no more than a couple of hours. Then what? I didn't want to go to the conclave; I didn't want strangers telling me what to do for the next one hundred years. That was madness.

Part of me wanted to give up, to slide down the door and cry but the other half wanted to run. How far could I get on one hundred and five pounds? Probably not even to Birmingham, and that was certainly not far enough. The king ruled Europe from his London residence and I couldn't get out of Europe without help. The only thing I could do was beg my parents for money to escape – if they were willing to help. After all, they had a good relationship with the king and their business depended on it; they might not want to jeopardise everything, even for their only daughter.

I sat down on my mattress. I must have been lost in my thoughts, because the next thing I noticed was my thin door flying off its hinges. The shitty piece of wood landed on the floor in the middle of my crappy flat with a whump.

I stood up. I knew what was coming; I'd sort of earned it, but he'd started it. Franklin and his goons stormed in. Franklin lunged at me and slapped me across the face so hard that I flew back two feet into the wall.

I held my face. It stung; even worse, my jaw felt loose – he'd knocked it out of joint. Pain zapped through me – but moments later my jaw reattached with an audible (and gross) snick. Super healing powers. Yep, those were kinda handy.

I pushed back from the wall as Franklin snarled at me, but his goons grabbed him and held him back. 'The king won't be happy if you harm her. He's vowed that you'll protect her for the next seven days,' a brown-haired hunk whispered urgently.

'Fuck off, John,' Franklin bitched, but he simmered down. 'You're going to pay for that stunt, bitch,' he snarled at me. 'After these seven days, you're anyone's game.'

'I already paid for it,' I bit back. 'You've already killed me. What else can you do?' I sniped.

He smiled, and it was not a nice smile. 'A lot, you stupid bitch. A lot. I'm going to enjoy making you scream – and not in a fun way.'

Ugh. If I'd been smarter I'd have stopped baiting him, but I was still angry – angry, lost and full of despair. I'd had another life planned for myself; my plans might have not been earth-shattering, but they'd been *mine*. Now I was trapped in a hundred years of bloody servitude to this wanker and his father. Why? Because I wanted to have a night out with my friends? Even a fool could see it wasn't worth the price.

How I yearned for time travel, to go back and stop earlier Bunny from going out drinking, but there was nothing to be done but to move forward. Somehow.

How was this jerk running around free whilst I was being forced into what amounted to indentured servitude? The system was wrong. It was broken. I had to find a way out and couldn't do it with this dumbass watching my every move.

I needed a plan.

Chapter 9

I tried to dial down my visible hostility to Franklin because he and his goons needed to think I was cowed. That was Part A of my new thought-up-on-the-fly plan. 'How long will you be staying here?' I asked as politely as I could manage.

Franklin glowered at me, sneering as he looked around at my – admittedly tragic – flat. It was a long way from the marble grandeur he was used to. How had I ever thought him handsome? He was less than average height, with mouse-brown hair and a weak chin. He was not my type. How had I ended up at a table snogging him? I shook my head. Stupid alcohol-induced poor decisions. I regretted every Jager bomb I'd done that night.

The taller of his two goons – John – answered. 'If you leave the flat, we have to follow you. But we don't need to stay if you'll agree to call us if you want to leave.' Hope flared. I could promise to call, and then just sneak out!

John finally let go of Franklin, who'd recovered his composure, and handed me a business card. 'Someone will be watching the building. If you leave without us, your seven days will be forfeit.' Hope died. Stupid, fickle hope.

I took the card. 'Fine.'

'I'm watching you. I'd love you to screw up – then I'll get you... permanently,' Franklin added, suddenly smirking.

I shuddered involuntarily. Permanently? What did that mean? Being alone with him for even one minute was reason enough to toe the line.

John stiffened at Franklin's jibe. I had the distinct feeling that he wasn't that fond of the vampire king's youngest son. Me neither, John; me neither. Maybe we could start a club.

'What about going out to take my rubbish to the bin?' I probed.

'That's acceptable, as long as you return immediately. Also, we can have items delivered if you require any food besides blood.' I guess vampires could eat actual real food then. I'd have to read their stupid manual later.

John continued, 'It would be best if you stayed in your flat.' This close, with the overhead light shining down on him, I saw John's eyes behind his dark glasses flick to Franklin.

Ah, it would be best to avoid the wanker. Got it. I really did. I nodded.

'We'll be outside until dawn. I'm John, this is Ethan.' He gave one of those manly head tilts to indicate the other goon.

'Thanks, John.'

They turned and left. My pathetic excuse for a door was still lying in the middle of the room, I looked at it and sighed. There was no saving it; that cheap thing should only have been used as an interior door anyway. It had torn at the hinges and had a gaping hole in it from being punched.

I picked it up and leaned it across the doorway. I only had one other neighbour on this floor, who rarely left her flat, but even so I wanted the little privacy I could get. Who knew how much I'd get after my seven days were up?

With no TV, no going out, and knowing that packing wouldn't take long, I settled on the sofa to read. I flipped open the vampire manual they'd handily supplied me with. *Chapter One: Blood: Why Do I Have to Drink It?* I checked the cover for the author – no name listed. It was a shiny paperback the size of a thin textbook. I had a lot of practice with textbooks, having recently completed my undergraduate degree in philosophy. News flash, no one wants to hire someone with a philosophy degree; it's a stepping-stone degree to further courses like studying law or something.

My mum thought a debutante didn't need a degree. I disagreed that I was a debutante. For a start I was probably too old, and also I wanted nothing to do with the snobs with whom my mother rubbed shoulders and shared air kisses.

I wondered if I should grab a highlighter for my little study session. This stuff was going to be important for the rest of my immortal life so it warranted being taken seriously, and nothing was more seriously academic than defacing your own copy of a book. Sure, I have an excellent memory, but fitting in at University had meant using highlighters. Even now, I clung to anything that would make me look normal, even in the privacy of my home. I got up and fumbled through my schoolbag, which was permanently slumped by the bed holding things I didn't have a place for.

I found a pink highlighter and sat back down. I highlighted the first line: *Blood is necessary for life. Blood is life. Don't forget.* I grimaced. Great. It was a manual written by someone who clearly – mistakenly – thought that they were funny.

The clawing hunger was enough of a reminder for me of how essential blood was. Speaking of which, it was starting again. I didn't want blood, though, I wanted hot food. I scanned the book for a mention of human food; the goons had mentioned ordering in, so surely vampires could eat...

Yes, you can eat human food if you want. You'll find that the desire to do so wanes over time, but until then eat what you want! You'll find things taste better, richer, and more flavourful. As your senses improve daily, so will your enjoyment of life.

The text was annoyingly upbeat. We would see.

Just remember that you can't eat without first ingesting blood. You can only gain nutrition from blood. If you try to eat without your daily recommended blood requirements, you'll be ill. You may drink, however.

Yup, my toast could attest to that.

I read the whole thing. It was depressingly unhelpful and filled with "filler" pages about how great "life" would now be. The manual was 90% pro-vampire propaganda. I turned the page and found the remaining pages listed recipes to make with blood. The first recipe was for a Bloody Mary. Everyone is a comedian. I rolled my eyes and tossed the book across the room. What a joke. I stood and paced the floor. I wasn't ready to face more blood yet, I just wasn't.

I'd asked about taking out the rubbish earlier because I really did need to empty my bins. I took off the hated dress, tossed it into the bin and put on my normal clothes. With nothing else to do and boredom already setting in, it was time to do a rubbish run. I tucked my phone into the waistband of my leggings, grabbed the rubbish bags and walked down the three flights of stairs and out to the alley.

I attempted to lift the lid of the bin, but it didn't budge. I couldn't see a lock on the front of it, so I looked around the edge. Someone had put a clamp on it. What the hell? Who would clamp a bin shut? I pulled the clamp off and tossed it on the ground. I lifted the heavy lid easily this time, I chucked in the first bag.

There was a sharp yip, and I dropped the lid in shock. That sounded like a dog.

I lifted the lid again and peered into the darkness. I couldn't see anything, but the scent of stale urine and rot assaulted my nose and made my eyes water. I found an abandoned crate, turned it over and stood on it. I flipped the bin lid again and pressed on the torch on my phone. Sure enough, a dog blinked up at me. Once he saw me, he let out a sad whine. My heart wrenched. Poor thing – someone had thrown him away.

I pushed myself up onto the rim and leaned over, balancing on my hips with my feet kicking out behind me. Then I reached for the dog. It was large-bodied but thin, and it weighed almost nothing as I lifted it. Then I realised that, thin as it was, I shouldn't have been able to lift it. Obviously, my strength was already increasing.

I could feel its bones under my fingers, and I was afraid that my slowly burgeoning vampire strength would crush it if I wasn't careful. It was so dirty and matted that I couldn't even tell what breed it was other than something large. It whimpered and cowered with its tail tucked between its legs and it wouldn't look at me.

My heart went out to it. I wasn't allowed pets in my flat, but I would only be there for a handful more nights and it wasn't like anyone ever inspected my apartment. Plus, this was an *emergency*. Feeling totally justified, I hoisted the dog over my shoulder and tucked my arm under its backside like a baby. I tossed in my last bag of rubbish and headed back upstairs, crooning nonsense to the scared creature that was quivering in my arms.

I had no dog food – or any food, for that matter. The bread was all gone, and the dog wasn't going to go for blood or mustard.

I dug out my phone again and called my captors.

'This is John,' he answered brusquely.

'John, I need some food. How do I order it?'

'Just tell me what you want.'

"Fine. I need tins of dog food, a loaf of bread, sandwich fillings, bacon, lettuce, cheese, eggs...' I rattled off a long list of items that would keep me and a whole other person fed and happy for seven days. It was petty, but I felt like I'd earned it.

While I waited for the food to be delivered, I carted the dog to the bathroom. There was a shower over the bath, and I started to run it. When the water was warm, I gently placed the dog in the bath and lathered him up with my shampoo. Dog shampoo would have been better, but anything would do. Dirt and clumps of hair swirled toward the drain. The poor thing looked like a drowned rat, and he was continuing to look at me like I was going to beat him.

He had medium-length hair, dark eyes and a fierce set of teeth. His coat looked dark, but it was still wet, so it was hard to say for sure. After two scrubs and a thorough rinse, I dried him gently with a towel and then brushed out his fur while blowing him dry with my hair dryer. He seemed to like the warmth and I wondered how long he'd been alone, out in the cold. Some people were just awful.

He was patient and quiet through the ordeal. By the time I'd finished, John had arrived with several bags of food. He raised his eyebrows at the dog. 'Was that creature here before?' he asked.

'Sure, Fluffy's been with me for years,' I lied easily.

'Hmmm.' He didn't buy it, but he didn't call me on it. John put the items on the table before leaving again. He moved the wrecked door aside before placing it back on his way out.

I looked at the newly named Fluffy. It was a name chosen on the fly, but it fitted him like Bunny fitted me.

Clean and dry, he no longer looked quite as thin and undernourished, but I knew the truth. I dug out a tin of dog food, emptied it into a bowl and put it on the floor. He wagged his tail, sniffed it – and gave me a distinctively dirty look.

I guess tinned food wasn't what he was used to, but it would have to do. I didn't know how an animal that was so obviously starving could turn up his nose. 'There isn't anything else,' I said firmly. 'Eat up.'

He sagged but gobbled it down without further ado. Once he was done, I rinsed his bowl clean, filled it with water and left it for him on the floor. The poor thing looked exhausted, and he was starting to sway. I coaxed him up on the sofa among my cushions and throws and he lay down with a doggy huff and curled in on himself.

Now that Fluffy was cared for, it was my turn. I grabbed the open bag of blood and poured the rest of it into a mug. I warmed it quickly in the microwave and chugged it down with my nostrils pinched closed. I hated how much better it made me feel but, even so, I still wanted something different.

I turned on the grill, popped a few rashers of bacon in it and made myself a bacon butty. Oh, if my mother could see me now; I was a long way from caviar and quail's eggs. Thank fuck.

Delighted when my stomach didn't revolt, I greedily gobbled down the sandwich. I put the kettle on and made myself a cup of decaf Earl Grey tea; it was one of the few things that I'd kept from my old life, back when I'd been what people had expected of me instead of who I really was.

I plugged my phone in to charge and snuggled with Fluffy while I drank my tea. I turned on the phone and started scrolling for similar breeds to see what he was. It didn't take long; now he was dry, his black-and-tan form was distinctive – he was a German Shepherd. I'd heard of them, but I'd never been allowed to have a pet when I was growing up so I didn't know much about dogs. I wondered why he'd been thrown away. Had he bitten someone? The breed looked fierce but

Fluffy had been nothing but gentle and patient with me. Poor guy.

I didn't have enough money for a vet visit, so I hoped being clean and fed would be enough for now. He leaned against me and started to snore gently. I smiled at him and petted his soft fur.

Maybe vamp life wouldn't be so bad if I had a pet. After Nana's recent death, I desperately needed something to love and it looked like Fluffy was it. And if those vampires tried to take him away from me – well, they were going to have to think again.

Chapter 10

Fluffy allowed me to escape my prison a little more since I had to let him out to do his business. John was sent for more dog items from the pet shop – a collar, lead, dog poo bags and some better-quality dog food for a large dog.

If he hadn't been sure that I hadn't had Fluffy before, he was now, but he seemed to be going along with it. Frankly, I was enjoying spending the vamp king's money. If I couldn't put together an escape plan, I'd be paying back every penny with my hundred years of indentured servitude so why not make some of it count? Fluffy was worth it.

The blood was going down a little better; it tasted good to me now and I felt stronger. My senses were sharper, and I had flawless skin – even my hair seemed thicker and shinier. I was still me, though, a gawky, skinny blonde with emerald-green eyes. But everything nice about me was enhanced. I'd become an attractive predator.

I wondered how ugly Franklin had been before he turned. He must have been bad because even now, with all the vamp advantages, he looked distinctly average. Beauty is in the eye of the beholder and all that, but Franklin was ugly inside and out.

Fluffy and I had been locked up for three days when I finally had a change in routine. John and Ethan showed up to replace my door, since Franklin had been the one to break it. I was smug when I was finally blessed with a real steel door with two deadbolts. I guessed even the bodyguards were concerned about the cheap door into my flat while they were responsible for my safety. The landlord would be thrilled when I left; I'd just added a hundred pounds a month to the rent with that door.

Unfortunately, Franklin was with John and Ethan. He glared at me, but I tried to ignore him. He didn't need to watch me so hard; I wanted him to think the

slap had truly cowed me. Maybe then he'd screw up –
and I'd be waiting.

Franklin sat on my sofa, so I was forced to perch on
the bed to get away from him. Fluffy trembled against
my side but forced a sad growl; I think he would have
tried to protect me if Franklin had tried anything. But
even if he'd been at full weight, my dog was no match
for a vampire; hell, in his current state he wasn't a
match for a strong breeze.

John and Ethan were surprisingly competent
handymen. They had power tools and some idea what
they were doing, so it didn't take them long to hang
the door. It closed better than it had when it was cheap
plywood, plus it felt solid.

I thanked them politely.

'You'll be making up for it once I get you,' Franklin
leered. I wondered again what I'd been thinking when
I hooked up with him at the club. Yuck.

John looked at him angrily, and Ethan looked away.
They must have seen the horror reflected on my face.
Would I be forced to work for Franklin? He was
disgusting.

'You'll service me in many ways,' he elaborated with a crude hand sign that made me gag. Oh hell, no. Even if I was forced to live and work in the vampire conclave, I wasn't signing up to be Franklin's little sex toy. Screw that.

John flushed red, his fists flexed, and I saw him struggle not to respond. Franklin watched him with a knowing smirk then met his eyes and quirked an eyebrow in challenge. John's jaw clenched, but he looked down and away. I felt bad for him – he had to work for that wanker and protect him. I gave him a sympathetic look.

I'd find a way out of this. Once they left, I was going to call my parents and ask if they'd give me enough money to get out of London, England, Europe – all of it – as soon as possible. I needed to put plans in motion; I was *not* going to belong to Franklin, not for all the tea in China.

Luckily, the men only stayed a few more minutes. Once they had left, I grabbed my phone. I called my dad first – he was less likely to ask questions.

He picked up on the third ring. 'Cyril Barrington, how may I help you?'

'Dad, it's me.'

'Bunny! What did I do to deserve this pleasure?' I pictured him running his free hand through his silver hair, a warm smile on his face.

'I miss you.' The words slipped out in a whisper as tears suddenly filled my eyes. Dad was Nana's son and so he was the closest I could come to her. He said some words with the same inflection as her and it tore at my heart.

'I miss you too, princess,' he replied jauntily, totally missing the tears in my voice. He wasn't the most emotionally attuned individual, but I did love him. 'We missed you at dinner the other night as well,' he said pointedly. 'Your mother was upset. You know how she feels about dinner parties. Will I see you at the wedding this weekend?'

'No, Dad. I don't think I'll be allowed to come.'

He was quiet a beat. 'Allowed? Why ever not, dear?' He sounded distracted; I imagined one of his multitude of assistants had just stepped in to hand him something to sign or initial.

'Didn't Mum tell you?' It was hard to keep the disbelief out of my voice. It had been *days* – how could she not have told him something so critical as his only child being turned into a vampire? By his business partner's son, no less.

I heard shuffling and voices. He did have someone in there. My stomach dropped and I was gripped by an overwhelming sadness. This was so important, and he wasn't paying any attention.

I waited at least thirty seconds before he finally spoke. 'Sorry, love, what didn't Mum tell me?' he asked.

'I was "accidentally" turned into a vampire,' I blurted out. 'I have to go work for them in their compound for the next one hundred years.' There was silence on the other end. 'Dad?'

'I'm sorry, love. It's quite a shock.' He paused. 'I'll talk to my associate.' Dad always referred to him as a 'business partner' or 'associate'; he never admitted what his partner really was – king of the vampires. And now my jailer.

I didn't have time for my father to make nice with the king. 'Dad, I need to get out of the country, and I can't go to Europe, either. I need to leave now. If I don't, I'll be more or less the property of his creepy son, the one that turned me. Will you help me?' I begged.

'Let me call him first, then I'll get back to you. I'm sure we can square this whole thing.' He paused. 'I'm sorry, love.'

I suppressed a sigh. 'Thanks, Dad.' Thanks for nothing. If anything, Dad was going to make things worse by flagging up that I wasn't as docile as I'd been trying to appear the last few days. Dammit.

He hung up and I felt even more lost. If Nana had still been here, not only would I already be halfway around the world, she'd have been with me.

The ache of loss filled my heart for the millionth time. Nana was my person, mother and grandmother rolled in one. She was my best friend as well. When I found out that she'd died and no one had told me she was sick, it had crushed me like nothing else. My parents hadn't told me because it was during my last week of finals at university, and they didn't want me to lose focus. Like anything could have been more important than being with her.

I felt the lump in my throat start to choke me. Sensing my distress, Fluffy gave a sharp bark and I knelt down to hug him. He snuggled under my chin and his warmth and love saturated me until I could shove the grief back down where it belonged and lock it away.

If no one would help me, I'd have to help myself. I was no damsel, dammit.

Chapter 11

I pulled out my ancient laptop, fired it up and started searching for ways to get the hell out of Dodge on the cheap. Before I got too far, Fluffy started to whine a little. He needed the toilet. 'It's still daylight, pal. Can you hold it?' He whined louder.

'Okay, okay, we'll come up with another plan.' I didn't have a cat litter box, not that he'd fit onto one, so I'd need to do something else. 'Come on,' I called as I went into the bathroom. Fluffy followed obediently. I picked him up awkwardly and held him over the toilet.

'Just go,' I said firmly. Fluffy looked at me. 'I know it's weird, but what else are we going to do? You could do this all by yourself, you know, once you're stronger. You're big enough.' I huffed. 'Just pee already. I can't hold you here forever.'

Fluffy obeyed, tinkling into my toilet, looking dismayed. 'It's not so bad,' I said encouragingly. 'It's what I do. And just think, it could be worse – it could be a bidet to spray water up your junk.'

Fluffy looked flustered, as much as a dog trying not to look at me could. There was a tentative knock on my door, and we were both grateful for something else to do. Since I'd engaged the two deadbolts, I had to set Fluffy down to answer it.

It was still daylight, so I was expecting a delivery person or my mum – not the woman on the other side.

'Isobel?' I asked my former schoolmate, frowning in confusion. 'What are you doing here?' My excellent memory meant I never forgot a face and I remembered hers well; she'd sat next to me in science lessons.

'You remember me!' Isobel clapped her hands together in delight.

'Of course I do. We were in school together for years and our parents are friends. Why wouldn't I remember you?'

She shrugged. 'I guess we moved in different circles. I didn't think you would.'

I had no idea why she was in my doorstep. I scrambled around for something else to say. 'You look great!' I said. 'The last time I saw you in that dress, it was at Eloise Winthrop-Smythe's eighteenth birthday party.'

She blinked weirdly at me, her mouth dropping open a little. I thought back over what I'd said. Had I been bitchy? Some people were weird about re-wearing clothes. I hadn't meant to be unkind, if she took it that way.

'You remember what I wore to a party five years ago?' she asked finally, dumbfounded.

'I have a good memory,' I said lamely. My weird memory always made people uncomfortable, so I often tried to hide it. People got jealous that I could see something once and remember it clearly. It helped at school; I was smart enough, but my prodigious memory saved my butt more than once after a night of bad choices rather than studying.

'Wow, that's so cool!' She seemed impressed. 'No wonder you got chosen.'

Had I been so self-involved that the people I'd grown up with thought I wouldn't remember them? Truthfully, I'd been really shy as a child; I'd had one friend and that was my Nana. I'd really liked Isobel and wanted her for a friend, but my parents only encouraged friendships and playdates with people above their social circle. Friendships with girls of an equal social standing like Isobel hadn't been encouraged.

'Chosen for what?' I asked blankly.

'Oh, um, can I come in?'

'Sure.' I ushered her in and shut the door. 'It's not much but it's mine,' I said weakly, waving at my tiny flat. 'How did you know where I lived?' I was curious about how and why she'd shown up at my door.

She looked away and glanced around. 'I work for the court.'

My blood ran cold. 'The vampire court?' I asked icily.

She froze at my tone. 'Yes,' she admitted and then she noticed Fluffy. 'Oh! You have a dog!' She rushed over and gave him a pat on the head. 'What's his name?'

'Fluffy.'

'Bunny and Fluffy! How cute!'

That's me, cute as hell. I smiled wanly. 'So are you a vampire too?' Wait, no, that couldn't be right because it was still daylight. Man, I was growing to hate daylight.

'Not yet.' She smiled. 'I've applied to be turned but there are all of these rules and prerequisites. How long did it take you?'

'I didn't want to be turned.' I crossed my arms. 'It was an accident.'

Her jaw dropped again. 'Oh my! Well, you are *so* lucky!'

I rocked back on my heels like she'd struck me. 'You aren't upset by the hundred years of servitude?'

She looked surprised. 'Heavens, no! I'll have a guaranteed job, a flat, and a life with other vampires. By the end, I'll have saved up a load of money. It sounds exciting! In a hundred years, I'll be able to go anywhere in the world!'

I thought she was overly excited. A hundred years was more than a lifetime and it seemed like forever to me. 'Oh, well, I hope you get accepted soon,' I offered, thinking she was insane.

'Yeah, me too! I had to lose the weight because you're frozen at your body size once you turn, and I want to look my best. I've lost ten kilos already,' she said proudly.

'Wow, that's great. I'm pleased for you.'

'Thanks so much.' She turned down the charm, cleared her throat and got serious. 'So, I'm supposed to get some information from you. That's my job – I do intake.'

'Intake?' I snorted. 'Vampirism isn't a job.'

She smiled again, 'I know. That sounds so stuffy when in truth we're being given immortality! What I do is more like induction into a new company.'

'So what do you need to know?'

She reached in her bag and pulled out a fancy tablet and a stylus. 'Okay. Full name.'

I frowned. 'Does it have to be my full name or what I want to go by?'

'I have to have your legal name for tax and government purposes, but we do have a line for your preferred name!'

I sighed. 'Elizabeth Octavia Barrington.'

She typed something into a form, I supposed; I couldn't see the screen of her tablet. 'I've always loved the name Octavia, it's so regal.'

'It's yours. Take it.'

She giggled. 'Preferred name.'

'Bunny Barrington.'

'Date of birth?'

'April sixth'

'Year?'

'You know this, Isobel, it's the same as yours.'

'Yeah, I guess I do!' She typed it in. 'Education.'

'MPhil.'

'University?'

'Edinburgh.'

'Oooh, you went to Scotland? How exciting! I've never gone further north than the Midlands!'

I shrugged. The truth was, it had been the best university I could find that was the furthest from my parents that they'd allow me to go.

She continued with the interview. It was extremely intrusive and thorough. By the time she was done, she knew everything about me but the colour of my underwear. Once we were finished, she thanked me and stood up. 'Oh, I'm supposed to give you this!' She handed me a gift card. 'It's a welcome gift to the life of being a vampire!'

I glanced down at it: it was a £50 gift card for the local teashop, black with gold lettering. I rolled my eyes. 'Hey, you're dead, enjoy a brew,' wasn't the greeting I'd expected. Once she'd left, I threw it in the bin.

Ten minutes later I took it out because – you know ... tea.

Chapter 12

Fluffy and I had three days left of restricted freedom and I was starting to panic. I still hadn't made a plan or gathered more cash. Dad hadn't called me back. Every time Franklin came around, he took every chance to leer and make lewd comments. I was looking for an escape.

So far, although I'd done copious research, I couldn't find a way to leave Europe for less than a hundred pounds. I was starting to look for au pair jobs, anything that would pay my way. I had a couple of prospects, but no one wanted a nanny for night-time only. I didn't have many job skills since the only job I'd had before was waitressing. I had a degree in the most worthless field ever, unless you wanted to discuss the meaning of life, which everyone knows is forty-two.

I could type, I could research, I could probably do lots of admin-type things, but no one wanted to take a chance on me. And absolutely no one wanted to send for me and pay my way to do it.

I shut my laptop and shoved it away. Thankfully night had fallen. 'Fluffy, let's go for a walk.'

He barked and wagged his tail in agreement. He was as tired of being locked up in a tiny room as I was. I texted John that I was taking Fluffy around the block and waited for the acknowledgement. Once it came, I pulled on a scarf and hat, attached Fluffy's collar and lead and we headed down the stairs.

At least Franklin had grown bored with babysitting me and now it was usually only John who showed up. How quickly the abnormal became normal. He met me at the bottom of the stairs. 'Evening, Bunny, Fluffy.'

'Hey, John. Are you alone again?'

'Yes.'

'Are you glad?' I asked with a grin. He smiled a little. 'Me too,' I said, and we shared a relieved nod.

'Where to? The park?' John asked.

I looked at Fluffy, who seemed to be following the conversation. At the mention of the park, his tongue lolled in a big doggy grin. 'Yes, it appears so!' I responded.

Fluffy always put me in a good mood. In the few days I'd had him, I was seeing his personality start to shine through. Without him, I would have been in the depths of despair but instead I was still optimistic. Maybe that last au pair application would come through, or Dad would get in touch with a plane ticket. It could happen. My glass was determinedly half full – admittedly of blood, but even so.

We left the building and walked towards the park. It was early evening, so people were still about, going home from work, shopping, dating. I looked on wistfully. That was my old life and I hadn't appreciated it enough. Now I was locked away, a danger to the community apparently, although I'd been sadly lacking in the urge to kill people – Franklin excepted. I didn't 'smell' everyone's blood or crave it.

I should have let everything go that I'd heard about vampires from the books and movies, but there had to be a reason for the hundred-year rule. Perhaps I was an aberration; maybe I just had the blood lust under control because I drank my three cups a day and ate real food? Maybe I was just a terrible vampire.

John was exceptionally quiet; he was quiet anyway, but today he was particularly laconic. I would have asked what was wrong but Fluffy was garnering a lot of admirers, with people asking to pet him or exclaiming over his handsomeness. He was a looker, and now that he was clean and fed, he was prancing with his head and tail held high.

While Fluffy was doing his business in the park, I finally had the chance to ask, 'What's going on? You aren't your usually gregarious self?'

John flashed me a look; he was *never* gregarious. He dug in his pocket and pulled out a few printed sheets. I took them cautiously, wondering what new torture would be facing me soon. 'Read it,' he ordered.

I obeyed. I read for a few minutes and when I had finished, I wasn't sure what to do. 'Is this possible? Would the king let me do this?'

John shook his head. 'No – and we'll both be in trouble if anyone finds out.'

I looked around but no one was paying attention to John, Fluffy or me. I looked at the pages again. It was the answer, my way out. 'But Alaska? Isn't it like ... the wilderness?'

John laughed. 'It's in a town. A town of supernaturals.'

I read the information again. It was a job – and not *just* a job either, because it offered housing *and* travel.

'Plus, it's dark all winter,' John went on. 'You won't be stuck inside all day.'

I hadn't thought of that. To be free for part of the year from the restraints the sun put on me? Heaven. I was growing excited. This was the answer. True freedom.

Could I do it? My mother and I had our issues, but could I leave her and Dad forever? I wouldn't be able to come back for at least a hundred years, and they'd be long gone by then. Of course, they'd be free to visit me. I wonder if my mother would lower herself to visit the 'colonies'?

I tucked the papers into the pocket of my jeans, excited and nervous in equal measure. This could be my ticket out of here. 'Thanks, John. I'm going to think about it.'

He gave me a nod, but his eyes showed disappointment.

'I won't let anyone know you gave me this,' I promised.

He grimaced before looking at me with regret. I hoped he wasn't worrying about the risk he was taking, because I'd take the information to my grave. After all, I might be there sooner than I expected.

We walked a little further and then it was time to go back. 'Why don't *you* take this offer?' I asked.

'Who says I won't?' he answered, but then he smiled sadly. 'I might someday, but for now I can't.'

He didn't elaborate, but I sensed a deep longing and knew there was a story he didn't trust me well enough to share.

Before he left me at the door to my apartment to go back to stand watch, he looked around and whispered, 'If you're going to do it, I need to know tomorrow night. I'll try to help you as much as I can.'

'Thank you. I'll let you know.'

Of course, all I did for the rest of the night was think about it. There were several jobs listed, all in the village of Portlock on the Kenai Peninsula Borough. I wasn't sure what that meant, but I looked over the various offerings.

The one I kept coming back to was for an admin assistant position to the local law-enforcement office. I'd always thought I'd make a good investigator – not that I had any training, but it was something that drew me. I mean, I'd solved my own death, right? Being there when it happened had helped, but still... I laughed a little at myself.

The salary wasn't impressive, but with housing and travel provided, any money I earned would be purely for food, savings, and fun. Plus, I'd be my own person: no indentured servitude. The bonus was that the only required skills were that the applicant could type, read, write and be supernatural, all skills I had mastered. Well, I was still mastering the supernatural part.

I frowned. I'd need to ask about blood availability. And what did other supernaturals think about vampires? Would that be a deal breaker?

There was an email address. I had no idea what time it was in Alaska, so I sent off a hurried message with my questions. As soon as I'd hit send my phone rang. Were they calling me already?

I looked at my phone screen; no, it was my father. I hurriedly swiped to accept the call. 'Hi, Dad.'

'Hi, Princess. How are you feeling?'

Like vampirism was an illness. 'Better than ever.' I fought to keep the sarcasm out of my voice as I flopped on the sofa. 'How are you?'

'I'm good. I spoke with my associate.' He paused.

After several moments, I prompted him to continue. 'What did he say?'

'Hmm? Oh sorry, I had another call. He said all is well.'

Hope rose inside me. If my heart had been still beating normally, it would have started racing. 'He'll let me go?'

'No, no, but he explained everything to me. This is a good thing! He'll take excellent care of you – for centuries, even.'

'What does that mean, Father?' All the joy I'd felt momentarily was seeping away. My own father was going to let me be enslaved for a hundred years?

'It means you'll be housed, have a job and, no, you won't be anyone's "indentured servant".'

My stomach flipped over as all my hopes died. 'Except I won't be allowed to leave ... or do anything I want to do with my life. That *is* indentured servitude because I'll have to work off my turning, blood and upkeep before I'm free.'

Dad sighed. 'Don't be dramatic, dear. It's no different to any other career – the only difference is that at the end of it you won't be old and tired. You'll still be young, and free to do whatever you wish. It makes perfect sense.'

'Will you or won't you help me escape?' I asked baldly.

'Where would you go?' he asked, his tone clearly indicating he was trying to pacify me. 'You have a good life here, a great offer, your family, your friends.'

'What friends?' The ones who had taken me drinking and let me leave with Franklin? Not a single one of them had messaged me; they were fair-weather friends, and the climate was currently stormy. 'Nana is gone. I won't be allowed to see anyone outside the compound, and I doubt anyone will visit.' That was cruel but I felt betrayed, as if my own father had sold me out to keep his business interests safe.

'Don't be silly, love. Your mother and I will see you all the time—'

'Will you send me money so that I can leave Europe?' I interrupted him.

Another heavy sigh. 'No, dear. I don't think that's in your best interests.'

Or his. 'So be it.' I hung up with a sob.

My own father would rather I was enslaved than help me fight for my freedom. I wiped away my tears and looked desperately for an email reply. Nothing. It was too soon.

I read the papers John had given me again. There was nothing holding me back now. I put in the web address and filled out the application: Bunny Barrington, assistant detective, had a nice ring to it.

Chapter 13

I tossed and turned all day. Finally Fluffy got sick of it and moved from his spot on the bed to the sofa. He'd adjusted surprisingly well to my reverse schedule – although I guess it was now my normal schedule. Anyway, he slept when I did and did his best to keep me entertained at night.

I kept getting up to check my email, although the vampire daytime exhaustion was real. Finally, I was rewarded:

Dear Ms Barrington,

Portlock is a very diverse community. Of course there are other vampires here, as well as many other types of supernaturals. I am a mermaid, but there are shifters and magic users of all kinds. We welcome fanged, furry and finned friends of all denominations.

We have a well-stocked blood bank of every type. Our community members love to help by donating frequently, and we have a dedicated supplier if one is required. There is also a wide variety of game and domestic stock if you prefer animal to human blood. We are proud to take care of our community in a thoughtful and practical way.

While it's true that during the winter it is dark a lot of the time, there are craftsmen and women who can provide daytime charms for the long summer hours. If you can commit to three years at the job you have applied for, we will provide a charm free of charge. We'll be looking forward to your application!

Thank you for considering Portlock, the little city with a big heart!

Sincerely,

Sidnee Fletcher

I read it through twice. Sidnee had such an upbeat voice, and I felt a little thrill of excitement zip through me. Daytime charms? I'd be able to see the sun again! After even a few days without it, the thought sent a zing of happiness through me. Was I really going to do it? Could I leave England? Frankly, after that letter and my dad's call, there wasn't much to hold me back. Now I desperately hoped that my application would be accepted because it was my only escape route. Of course, there was the small matter of getting out of London without my captors being any the wiser, but I'd worry about that when I heard back about the application. With that thought, I was finally able to fall asleep.

I was awakened by Fluffy barking fiercely and my door banging open against the wall. I jumped out of bed in my underwear and a sleep shirt and searched around desperately for something I could use as a weapon.

Franklin came storming in. I backed away as far as I could, but he ran at me snarling, his fangs on display and murder in his eyes. 'How dare you, bitch!'

I was against the sink and had nowhere else to go. His hand wrapped around my throat, and he sprayed spittle over my face.

Fluffy snarled and bit Franklin's leg to try to pull him off me. Franklin kicked him across the room and my poor dog's body hit the wall with a loud thud and crumpled. I gasped, but I couldn't get enough air to do more than that. My heart ached and I was terrified that the bastard had killed my hound.

'I let you have your nights!' Franklin yelled. 'I've put up with your attitude and even with you kneeing me in the balls, but I'm not going to let you make a fool out of me!'

I had no idea what he was talking about. I hadn't done anything. As he released my throat slightly, I gasped, 'What are you talking about?'

Franklin pulled a sheaf of papers from his jacket pocket and shoved them in my face. It was my email exchange with Sidnee. 'How did you get those?' I asked. My mind immediately went to John. Had he betrayed me, set me up?

'You seriously can't believe we let any new vampires go unmonitored?' he sneered. 'We keep the community safe from baby vamps like you.'

They were monitoring me, but how? A bug on my computer or something? Why hadn't I even considered that? Surely, there were other 'accidentally' turned vamps – I couldn't be the first vampire that didn't want a hundred years of servitude. I doubted they had much trouble with vampires that had applied and knew up front what the rules were.

'What have I done that's so bad? I'm not a danger! You're a bigger danger than I am!' I argued righteously.

Franklin lunged at me, teeth bared, and I knew he was going to tear my throat out. Luckily, John and Ethan had finally come through the door, and they yanked him back in time.

'Stop, mate!' Ethan shouted. 'Calm down. You know that this is the daughter of your father's business partner. He isn't going to forgive you easily for killing her.'

'My father had no problem with me turning her!' Franklin snapped back.

John's eyes flicked to me.

'He didn't?' I asked, confused. Why didn't Franklin get in trouble? The king wouldn't have been doing his job if he allowed random people to be turned – or, even worse, killed.

'Of course not, you bitch,' he sneered at me, *schadenfreude* shining in his eyes. 'I was hired to bite you.'

I was so stunned that I slid down and sat on the floor. 'What?' I looked at John for confirmation, but he was looking as surprised as me.

Ethan glanced at me sheepishly before looking away. He'd known.

'Who hired you?' I asked faintly. Who would want a no one like me as a vampire? And why? It made no sense.

Franklin looked chagrined; I had the distinct feeling he hadn't meant to let that little detail slip. I seemed to have a way of getting under his skin, probably because he knew how much I hated him. He stalked over and picked me up. He set me on my feet and let me go. I stood awkwardly, shying back from him as far as I could. My eyes flicked to Fluffy – God, he still hadn't moved. If he was dead, I couldn't take it. I was going to implode.

Franklin put his finger in my face. 'If you tell anyone what I said, I'll kill you.' He spoke the words quietly and evenly, and it was far scarier than the times he'd ranted and raved at me.

I swallowed hard; I believed him. His lust for me had turned to hatred partly because of the bollock-injury, partly because he was being forced to babysit me. Now, to add insult to injury, I knew something that I wasn't supposed to. Someone had got approval from the king and had hired Franklin to turn me into a vampire. The whole thing was no accident at all. Who could possibly hate me so much?

Franklin backed away from me and turned to leave. Ethan and John followed him.

'How much!' I yelled after them. 'How much did you get to do this to me?' I couldn't keep the sob out of my voice.

He turned and gave me a slimy smile. 'Fifty grand. Not much at all.' The look on my face must have satisfied him because his smile widened as he turned on his heel and left.

The second the door shut, I scrambled over to Fluffy and put my hand on his stomach to see if he was breathing. His tummy rose and fell; his breathing was shallow and hard to monitor under his fur but thank fuck he was alive. I breathed a sigh of relief as I gathered him up and sank onto the sofa, holding him and waiting for his eyes to open.

'Fluffy, wake up!' I begged as my tears fell on his fur. He stirred. 'Come on, Fluffy!' I entreated. 'Come on, boy!'

His eyes opened and he looked at me and whimpered. He squirmed and I released him. He jumped down awkwardly, more a slide to the floor, but he landed on his feet. He stumbled a little, but then he walked around and barked at me. I slumped in relief. He seemed all right; the kick must have just stunned him.

'Are you okay, little man?' I asked.

He pranced and trotted about and gave another single bark. I ran my hands over him. Everything seemed to be in the right place, no broken ribs. When he jumped back up on the sofa, I stroked him gently in case he was bruised. He lay down next to me and snuggled into my side as I leaned my head back and closed my eyes.

Who would have done this to me? I hadn't known that anyone felt that strongly about me. Maybe the wankers I'd dumped the drinks on? The timeline fit and they'd been extremely angry, plus they had money. But fifty thousand pounds? That was *real* money. Who had that to burn? I grimaced. Most of the trust fund kids I'd grown up with would think fifty grand was nothing. I had a huge suspect pool.

I guess my delighted thought that I'd solved my own murder was horribly wrong. I hadn't: Franklin may have done the deed, but he was nothing more than the instrument. And a blunt one, at that.

Someone wanted me dead, eternally so. Why? I couldn't fathom it. I was too much of a waste of space for someone to care enough to kill me yet someone had, someone with money, connections and a deep hatred of me.

I had an enemy.

Chapter 14

As I sat with Fluffy, I heard the text tone on my phone beep. I sighed. What was even the point of checking it? I didn't want to hear from my family or the vampire court, but I suppose it might be John. I heaved myself up and picked the phone up off the table.

I swiped it open and clicked the text. It wasn't from anyone I knew. I squinted at it and figured it was a phishing scam, but out of sheer boredom I opened it.

Hello! Your application has been received. If you are still interested, reply with a Y for yes and we will schedule an interview. Congratulations!

Was the court monitoring my phone as well? I looked around suspiciously, then I rolled my eyes at myself; they weren't actually here right now. It seemed likely that they had hacked my phone but what did I have to lose? If I replied, maybe I might still have an opportunity to get away if I had a job to go to.

I typed a Y and hit send. An auto reply hit my inbox a few seconds later. *Thank you for your interest! You'll receive a call within three hours.*

Wow, they didn't mess around. I stared at the phone for a few minutes more before double-checking the sound was up, then I put it down. Failing to prepare was preparing to fail; ugh, I could even hear mum's prissy voice saying that inside my head.

I decided I might as well get dressed; although I wouldn't be visible during a phone interview, it would make me feel better. Trying not to wake up Fluffy, I slid out from under him. He gave a little groan, stretched, but didn't wake.

I dressed and went into the bathroom to brush my hair and teeth. My hair was snarled from sleep, so I brushed it out gently and braided it down my back. Long, thick and straight, my hair is one of my favourite attributes – even more so now that it had extra lustre thanks to eternal life.

I didn't shower because I didn't want to miss the call, but I should have done because it turned out I had plenty of time. Once dressed, I scrambled some eggs to have with my very real Bloody Mary. I even used the damned manual's recipe. I'd needed the extra blood to calm down my nerves, and blood, vodka and Worcestershire sauce turned out to be incredibly delicious.

Feeling calmer, I went online to see if I could figure out who'd hired the vamps to turn me. Someone had spent some serious money to screw up my life, and I needed to know who and why. Maybe my parents had enemies I didn't know about. Maybe this was all to fuck up a deal between my dad and the king? Maybe the objective had been to make Dad angry and open up an opportunity for someone else to step into his business shoes. I didn't really know what the king and Dad did together, but I knew it made Dad millions. Money is a huge motivator, right?

On my 'other suspects' list, I had the idiots I'd dumped the drinks on, but I didn't know their names or how to locate them. It seemed a bit extreme to kill someone just because of a little spilt liquid, but people killed each other over road rage, so it could definitely be possible. They were still at the top of my list because I really didn't have many enemies. I didn't have many friends, either. What a shit time to discover I inspired apathy in people. *If I got to Portlock, that was going to change*, I vowed to myself.

I'd had the usual childhood dramas, a few sour exes, but no one who had the money for this. I found it hard to accept that I'd aroused the level of hatred that hiring an assassin would surely require.

How could I solve my murder while I was stuck in this flat with three guards? The furthest I could go was the park, and that was when I was being supervised. To investigate the handsy-men, I'd have to go back to the restaurant from which I'd been fired. Maybe I could convince John that I'd left something there. I probably did have a final pay cheque, but it couldn't have been much once the drinks I'd dumped had been deducted. Truthfully, I probably owed the restaurant – I'd only earned two days' pay and that had been a lot of expensive drinks.

Loath as I was to admit it, Franklin was probably the easiest lead to follow. I just needed to trick him into spilling more of his secrets.

Chapter 15

The phone rang and I jumped. I ran to pick it up and swiped it open. The number showed an American code.

'Hello? May I speak with Ms Barrington?'

'Yes, that's me,' I said a bit breathlessly.

'Ms Barrington, this is Sidnee Fletcher. Do you have time to complete an interview?'

Sidnee Fletcher, I placed her name instantly. 'Sidnee Fletcher the mermaid?' I blurted.

There was a pause then a laugh. 'Yes – although I don't usually get greeted that way!'

I blanched; I couldn't believe I'd just said that. 'I'm so sorry. I've never met other supernaturals besides vampires and I'm not sure of the protocol. And yes, I have time for the interview now.'

'No worries! Hold on and I'll connect you. Oh, and Bunny?'

'Yes?' My stomach dropped; maybe I'd already blown it.

'Good luck. I already like you!'

As I thanked her, hold music started playing and I waited. It wasn't long before a loud, booming male voice blasted out at me. I moved the phone away from my ear and turned down the volume. 'Ms Barrington, this is Nomo Gunnar Johansen.'

He said Nomo like it was a title or a species. 'Nomo? Is that a type of supernatural?' I hazarded a guess.

A quick bark of laughter. 'No, ma'am. Nomo is a title. I'm the head of all law enforcement for Portlock. You'll be working directly under me.'

'Oh, right. Sorry!'

'Not a problem. Now, let's see. This role is for an administrative assistant. What kind of experience do you have with typing forms and filing?'

Good grief, I was going to fail! I had zero experience. 'Umm, I have to tell you, Mr Johansen, that I don't have a lot of experience, but I am an excellent writer.

I can type sixty words per minute without errors. I do know how to alphabetize, so I don't think filing will be a problem.'

Oh man: 'I know how to alphabetize'? That was basically saying I knew the alphabet song, I needed to pull something else out of the bag. I cleared my throat. 'I'm very personable and I'm excellent on the phone. As you can see.'

'Indeed.' He sounded amused. 'Organisational skills are a must. How are you at that?'

This felt like a very informal interview, and I wondered if Mr Johansen was organised enough to have a list of questions.

'I am very organised,' I promised. I looked around at my flat and grimaced. I *could* be very organised; it wasn't *impossible* – just not probable.

I could hear a pen scribbling over paper.

'You said you're a vampire. Have you completed your required years of service?'

My heart sped up, which was scary since it was beating a lot slower than it used to do before I was turned. I felt panic rising. Why couldn't I escape the damned conclave? I could lie, but it would be easy enough to check. One call to the king and it would all be over.

Tears welled up. The truth, then. 'No,' I admitted. 'I was attacked and turned against my will. I haven't completed the hundred years – I've only been a vampire for five nights.' The truth was raw and embarrassing, but I hoped it would curry me some sympathy, if nothing else. I needed every advantage I could get.

Silence. More scribbling. Then, 'One moment, Ms Barrington.' Nomo's tone was now deadly serious.

More music. I wiped my eyes. Without money or this escape, I was doomed. I'd be in the conclave, stuck at Franklin's beck and call. I sat next to Fluffy; even though he was still asleep. I needed the comfort of his soft fur. I ran a hand over him gently.

The hold music clicked off. 'Ms Barrington?'

'Yes?' I said quietly, sadly.

'Not a problem. You fall under code 381.7 in the vampire code book. Accidental turns, and other turns without prior application or authorization, are free to choose their communities. You'll still be under the observation of our vampire liaison to the Nomo office, but there's no impediment to your move. I'll have the visas drawn up within forty-eight hours. Your travel documents should be on the way by the end of the working day. Do you have a passport?'

'Yes, of course!'

'Good. Congratulations! I look forward to working with you.'

I was stunned. I must have been quiet a few moments too long, because Mr Johansen continued, 'Are you there, Ms Barrington?'

'Yes!' I cleared my throat and cast around for something intelligent to say, 'Sorry, I was thinking about my dog. Would it be acceptable to bring him?' Fluffy stirred awake at that and sat up, giving his tail three happy taps.

'Sure, we like dogs in Alaska.'

'He's rather large.'

'Not a problem.' There was a chuckle on the other end. 'Do you accept the job offer?'

'Oh – oh, yes of course! And call me Bunny. I'm very excited! Thank you so much.'

He laughed again. 'You are very welcome. See you soon. And Bunny?'

'Yes?' I said cautiously.

'Welcome aboard! Portlock is excited to have you.' He hung up.

I looked at the phone for a moment then I knelt down beside Fluffy and grabbed his face. 'Fluffy! We are going to Alaska!'

Fluffy barked excitedly. Maybe Fluffy was ready for a change too.

Chapter 16

I texted John to let him know that I was taking Fluffy outside. I found the dog lead and snapped it on.

Clear, John texted back. I wonder if he was going to give me more information tonight, or if Franklin was watching him too closely. I shrugged and put on my jacket to head down.

At the door to the building, I looked around, but I couldn't see John, Ethan, or Franklin. The cold night air whipped around me, and I felt a prickle of foreboding. I turned the corner to walk around to the grassy area at the back of the building where Fluffy obligingly took care of his business. We were coming back across the parking area when Franklin came charging at me with Ethan and John in tow.

'That's it, you've lost the last of your freedom,' he started once he was in earshot. He was smirking, triumphant.

I reeled back. 'What?'

'You're a stupid, scheming little twat. You're trying to run out on your hundred years and embarrass the court. When I tell him what you've done, my father is going to give you to me as a prize. I'm actually pleased you took the bait, you stupid bitch.'

'Bait?' I looked at John in disbelief, who looked away and down. Son of a bitch. He *had* set me up. Regardless, he was visibly unhappy about his role in it. I wasn't too thrilled about it either.

'You think John would be allowed to lure our baby vampires away? We *own* him.'

I felt the blood leave my face and brain and I thought I was going to faint. Was Alaska a set-up? Was Johansen and Sidnee in on it? Was it all bollocks? What kind of elaborate game were they playing? Fluffy leaned against my leg, trembling. How could I protect him if we were locked up with this monster?

I looked at John again. His jaw had tightened at the word 'own', and for the second time I wondered what his story was. The material he'd given me had to be real. I'd talked to an overseas number; Nomo Johansen was real; Sidnee was real. They had to be.

I tried to think but Franklin wasn't giving me any time. He grabbed my arm and started pulling me towards the building. 'Pack your shit. You have four hours and then we're out of here.'

I yanked my arm away and pulled Fluffy behind me so no one would be tempted to kick him again.

'John, you're on duty. I'll be back at...' Franklin glanced at his watch '...11:07. Have her ready.' He stormed over to the black Mercedes. Ethan climbed in after him and the driver pulled away.

Once we were alone, I turned to John. 'You set me up?' I'd meant for it to come out accusingly, but it instead I sounded hurt.

'I'm very sorry.'

'Was any of it real? The job?'

He looked away. 'Yeah, it's a real place, I just had to get you to go for it so Franklin would get his own way.

He's a scumbag. I'm sorry, but he's holding a lot over me.'

I wanted to be angry with him, but ultimately he was in the same boat as me; stuck unwillingly in vampire schemes. I sagged, defeated.

John followed me back into the building and up to the flat. 'After Ethan drops off Franklin at home, he'll bring back boxes and a pet carrier.'

I nodded. I had a couple of suitcases, so I started packing my clothes and toiletries. Everything I wanted or needed went in there; if I had a chance to escape, I'd take it with or without my luggage but I'd prefer the former, so I'd still have the things I cared about. But at that point, I'd just have been happy to have Fluffy; everything else was just trappings.

Chapter 17

Sorting through my paltry belongings only took an hour. Ethan came by and dropped off the boxes and a large, plastic, pet carrier for Fluffy, who eyed it dubiously when I set it down by the door.

It took little time to pack the rest of my stuff; I didn't have much in the way of kitchen items, and even less in decor. When I was done, the apartment was bare of everything but the bed, the table, the nightstand and the sofa. Since those had come with the flat, I was done. My meagre possessions could be hauled down in short order.

As I set the last box by the door, my phone beeped with an incoming text. It was my travel itinerary from Sidnee. I scanned through it. Wow – business class from Heathrow to New York, Seattle then to Anchorage, Alaska. After that I couldn't find the class of flights. But I'd go from Anchorage to Homer to Portlock. It was going to be one hell of a long trip.

Since I could only fly at night I was stopping for a day in New York, and then in Anchorage, at vamp-friendly hotels with blood on tap. Nomo Johansen had thought of everything. I suppose it had been too difficult to get me one of those charms before I was in Alaska. Maybe they had geography limits.

God, I wanted to be free so much. I'd be the best damned administrative assistant in the world – if I could just get to Portlock. I glanced up at John. 'Help me, John, please,' I begged.

He frowned. 'I can't. They'll destroy me. For some reason, the king badly wants you under his control.'

It was my turn to frown. I couldn't imagine why. Sure, he was my father's business partner, but they were doing well, and I'd never heard of any problems between them. Dad clearly admired the king – he was willing to hand over his only daughter to his care.

'I could be free,' I hissed urgently. 'I got the job – the one you showed me. I just need to get on the plane without being stopped.'

sounds easy, but whatever you have on your phone they have too. They *know*, Bunny. You can't escape.'

Telling me I couldn't do something was like igniting rocket fuel. I was even more determined. 'You don't have to do much, just look away for a minute, long enough for a cab to pick up Fluffy and me.'

'Even if I do that and take the punishment, they'll stop you before you get out of the cab on the other side.'

I sensed he was giving in, so I pushed harder. 'But I want the chance.' I paused. 'Please, John. I can't give up now. I'm so close. I could be free.'

He froze then a muscle in his jaw twitched. It was the last word that had done it – he wanted freedom too. 'Alright, I'll call a cab from my phone, then they won't know when it will turn up.'

'Thank you so much.' I threw my arms around him, and he patted me awkwardly. I let him go and he punched in a number and ordered me a taxi. Freedom was so close, I could taste it.

Chapter 18

I coaxed Fluffy into the large dog carrier. He gave me a baleful look, but he didn't bark in protest. I grabbed the carrier, which was nearly as large as I was, and John picked up my three bags. We hurried down the stairs and out to the front of the building.

We didn't have to wait long; it was well after dark and most people had already gone to wherever they were going. 'Get through security as quickly as you can,' John advised, 'They can't touch you once you're through.'

I nodded. 'Okay, I will. Thank you, John.'

The cab driver loaded the bags into the boot as I shoved Fluffy's carrier onto the seat and climbed in after him. John watched me drive away with a heartbroken expression. He wanted to be in the cab too, running away. I wanted that for him as well, but the tickets and visa were only for me.

'Thank you,' I mouthed to him, and he smiled mournfully as I sped away.

The drive to the airport was uneventful but my breath caught every time a car passed us or I heard a random siren. I was on edge, fearful of something going horribly wrong, of Franklin catching up with me. He knew my flight details and once he realised I'd gone, it would be a fight against the clock.

Once we neared the turn-off to the terminal, the cabbie asked, 'Which airline?'

'British Airways, please.' Seconds later, we were pulling alongside the curb. John had already paid the driver, so I grabbed a trolley and shoved all my bags and the dog carrier onto it.

It was late and the baggage check-in queues were almost non-existent. At the checkout I weighed and checked in my bags quickly. With the bags all done, the attendant looked at Fluffy. 'Vet's certificate?' she asked.

Panic jolted through me. I held her eyes and hoped the panic in them would convey my desperation. 'I don't need that!' I blurted. My teeth snapped down. Not now, incisors! I pulled my lips over them and tried to calm myself down.

She blinked slowly at me before nodding once. 'You don't need that,' she repeated, her tone monotonous. She blinked again and gave me a normal smile. 'Let's get your puppy checked in.' Holy Shit! What had I just done? Did I have Jedi mind powers? I reluctantly parted with Fluffy, who would be stored in the hold.

I heard a kerfuffle behind me. I looked over my shoulder and spotted Franklin. Shit!

I ran forward towards the entrance to passport control, skidding on the hard, tiled floors of Terminal 3. I looked behind me and saw Franklin was running at me with some vampires I'd not seen before. I hoped John was okay.

I've been called skinny my whole life. While I do have a good metabolism, I'm mainly thin because I'm a runner; I was a sprinter at university, and I did well.

I ran with every ounce of energy I could muster. I was ready to do the same again.

I made it to the queue for security but there were a lot of people waiting. Anxiety tore through me. Maybe Franklin wouldn't make a scene; maybe being in line was enough to protect me... That was all I had time to think before I was snatched out of the queue. I squeaked in surprise then a hand covered my mouth. I was dragged into the nearest men's toilets.

'You're mine,' Franklin growled. His fetid breath was hot against my ear, and he followed his words with a disgusting lick.

I shuddered.

'We're going to walk out of here and you're not going to make a sound.' He pulled a knife from his pocket and jabbed it far enough into my ribs to break the skin. There was a warm, trickling sensation down my side. 'Got it?'

I nodded, afraid that if I took a deep enough breath to answer or scream the knife would puncture something I needed.

'Walk,' Franklin ordered.

I walked.

I wanted to cry and scream. I'd been so close to freedom... And Fluffy, Fluffy was in the plane's hold, waiting for me, thinking everything was fine. I couldn't leave without him! But he'd be free in Portlock ... maybe it was better to let him take the flight without me. Would he be sent onwards if I didn't board the plane?

A few people looked at Franklin and me curiously as we made our way out of the toilets, but nobody stopped or asked if I needed help. So much for airports being a safe space. Franklin pushed me out of the door to his waiting goons – two of whom were holding John.

John wouldn't look at me. He was standing strangely as if he was in pain. With his powers of vampiric healing, it must have been an awful attack if he was still hurting. I wanted to apologise to him, but I didn't want to get him into deeper shit by indicating that he'd had a role in my escape. They might be operating on the assumption that he was just incompetent.

The knife left my side, and I took a deep breath. Franklin switched his grip from my arm to my hair and propelled me towards his black Mercedes. I balked and tried to pull back, but he was controlling my head and I couldn't break free.

If I got into that car, my life was over.

One of Franklin's goons hurried over and opened the door. Franklin tried to shove me in the car but I resisted, begging John with my eyes for one last bit of help. He was still standing between some of the other vampires, but they weren't holding him. He stared intently at me, but I couldn't understand what he was trying to convey.

Suddenly he surged forward. The vampires next to him were surprised and acted too slowly. John grabbed the back of Franklin's suit jacket and yanked him off his feet. The knife flew up in the air and I caught the glint of it as the lights reflected off the blade. Without thinking, I reached up and grabbed it as it fell back down. The hilt landed in my palm, and I grasped it tightly.

The other henchmen had caught John and pulled him back. Franklin punched him and John doubled over with an 'oof'. Franklin whirled back to me; his face twisted in ugly, towering rage. I stepped back but I didn't have anywhere to go except into the car – and no way was I getting in there voluntarily. Franklin raised his fist. He was going to punch me and knock me out. If I let that happen, I might as well die.

I took a step towards him. As his fist came forward, I closed my eyes, jammed the knife into his crotch with all my might and gave it a savage twist. His fist clipped my ear, making it ring, and I stumbled and nearly fell.

Franklin gasped as his hands came down protectively over his groin, but it was too late. Blood was spurting through his hands. I'd hit his femoral artery.

I locked eyes with John as one of other minions released him to run to Franklin's side. He threw Franklin in the car and the car sped away. The wheels squealed as they left.

'Go,' mouthed John.

I looked around. The remaining vampires were in shock, staring after Franklin's speeding car. I took my chance and ran back into the building.

Chapter 19

I found the nearest ladies' toilet and hastily cleaned up; security wouldn't let me stroll through covered in blood and I had plenty of it on my hands and my clothes. Luckily, I had a change of clothes in my backpack, so I hurriedly washed my hands and changed. I shoved the soiled clothing in the bin then emerged cautiously, looking for my pursuers. No one.

I headed to security for a second time. This time, the queue was far shorter. I blended in, keeping my head down except for glancing frequently around me. My heart was hammering as I approached the front of the queue. Safety was only inches away. As I was called forward, I nearly sobbed with relief. I wouldn't even care if they wanted to cavity search me.

They didn't, luckily, and I was soon through security, hopping as I pulled on shoes one-handed in my haste. Once my backpack had been reclaimed and I was through, I took a deep breath. They couldn't get me now without involving the airport police.

I'd done it. I'd really done it, but only a fool would relax just yet.

I headed straight to my gate – with all the dicking around, the boards said that the plane would be boarding in five minutes. By the time the goons drove Franklin to the hospital or to the vampire court, I'd be safely in the air. Vampires heal quickly but I'd done some real damage. Franklin was vain enough to want to make sure everything was working properly *down there.*

They were boarding by the time I arrived at the gate, so I walked straight on and took my seat in the third row in business class. I sank down gratefully, hunched against the window and buckled my seatbelt. Boarding continued for a while but eventually trickled to a stop. I had headphones, inflight entertainment and even a blanket, but I wasn't relaxing until we were in the air.

I kept begging silently for them to close the doors, but they stayed open. I closed my eyes, the tension building inside me until I wanted to scream, 'Let's fucking go!'

A flight attendant tapped me on the shoulder. I shrank back and stared at her. This was it. They'd called and I was going to be arrested.

'Champagne, water or orange juice, ma'am?'

'Do you have any tea?'

'Hot drinks will be served when we're under way ma'am. Can I get you a cold drink in the meantime?'

'Champagne would be great.' The alcohol might help settle my raging nerves.

'Of course.' She gave me a wide smile and passed me a glass of cool sparkling wine. I took a calming sip and wished the glass was bigger.

Finally, the doors closed and I almost sobbed with relief. I'd really done it. I was safe.

Chapter 20

We flew in darkness to New York and I spent the day in a tiny windowless hotel room. I couldn't have cared less about the size of the room – I was free! The Nomo had arranged everything for me, including blood deliveries, and care for Fluffy. That day I slept the best sleep I'd had in a week.

The following day, I arrived in Anchorage, Alaska and was reunited with Fluffy. We stayed in a tiny, dog-friendly B&B until the evening, when we headed back to the airport for the next leg of our journey.

When I arrived at the gate for Ravn Air, I was surprised the plane had propellers. Who knew people still flew around in those?

It was only a forty-five-minute flight, but both Fluffy and I were tired of travelling. On top of that, I was growing anxious. I was free but I was also alone in a foreign country and unable ever to go back home. I hadn't even said goodbye to my parents.

I'd made an enemy for life in Franklin, which wasn't my wisest move – but there again, tangling with him to start with hadn't been my best choice. I frowned. Wait a minute... Didn't vampires have some sort of ability to cast a thrall on their victims? If Franklin had been hired to turn me, drinking with him that night probably hadn't been a bad decision on my part but a deliberate plan on his. Son of a bitch.

Now that I was out of the clutches of the vampire king, Franklin and his minions, I was terrified for new reasons. What if the residents of Portlock were disappointed in my lack of typing skills and sent me back? What if I failed and was cast out? What if – and this was the worst one – what if the vampire king sent someone after me?

With all sorts of anxieties churning in my gut, we landed in Homer. As I walked into the tiny airport building, I looked around in shock. The aircraft I'd come in on was the biggest one there. When I asked for my flight to Portlock, the lady behind the information desk pointed out my new plane. It was tiny; it didn't look big enough to carry Fluffy, let alone me, a pilot and my luggage. 'I'm flying in that?' I squeaked.

She smiled kindly at me. 'First time in Alaska?' she asked.

'Yes.'

'You're from the UK?'

'London.'

'Well, in Alaska you'll be flying bush planes more often than 737s. They're perfectly normal and safe.'

'Will it hold me and all my stuff?' I asked dubiously.

She was kind enough not to laugh. 'Sure will, honey.' She examined me with a critical eye. 'You can't weigh more than a hundred and thirty soaking wet.'

I wasn't sure exactly what that meant – I weigh 63 kilos, 65 after a pizza binge – but I got her drift. I wasn't a large lady.

'Head on out,' she said. 'The pilot's ready for you.'

I walked out clutching Fluffy's carrier in front of me like a shield. The plane had four seats and the pilot was shoving my luggage into the compartment behind one of them. Once he was done, he helped me up and placed Fluffy on the seat next to me.

My face must have reflected my inward terror because he smiled and said, 'Don't worry, lady. I haven't wrecked a plane yet.' The "yet" wasn't as reassuring as he'd probably intended.

'Really?'

'Really. I'm Jim.' He reached out a hand.

I took it. 'Bunny.'

'Alright, Bunny, let's fly.'

Chapter 21

It was surprising that Jim hadn't commented on my unusual name, I was almost disappointed. I'd had an elaborate tale ready about how I'd acquired the nickname, involving an eagle and a cliff edge.

Jim handed me a set of headphones in case we needed to communicate. I put them on as he climbed into the front seat and did all of his piloty things. When the engine started, it was so loud that I suddenly understood the need for headphones. I wished I had something for Fluffy's ears.

As we taxied down the runway and lifted into the air, I looked for something to hang onto. I didn't see anything, so I clutched the sides of my seat. I hoped Fluffy wasn't too scared. When I gazed into his carrier he was lying down, and I couldn't tell if he was relaxed or terrified. He'd travelled well so far but this was loud and bumpy. I laced my fingers through the mesh, and his nose nuzzled against my fingers. He was okay.

It was a while before I was able to relax and enjoy the ride and the stunning scenery. Alaska felt immense and wild. Even in the darkness, my vampire vision showed that we were passing over miles of nothing but trees, water and empty land. There were no lights, no signs of civilisation; it was both intimidating and freeing, and it was a world away from the busy lights of London.

After some time, Jim said, 'Bunny, we're almost there. We have to pass through the barrier. It's a bit bumpy but that's perfectly normal. Are you good?'

I nodded, but I was lying. Bumpy didn't sound good. And what was the barrier? Now didn't feel like a good time to ask questions; I wanted Jim focused on the damn plane. My tension increased and I clutched the sides of my seat again as we started to bump through some pretty wild turbulence.

The plane dropped and bounced, doors rattled, and my stupid fangs dropped because I was trembling so hard, but finally we were through. I let out an explosive breath of relief.

I could see the town below us. From the air it looked neatly organized and I could see the airstrip clearly next to the water, but instead of landing there Jim headed for the water itself. Thinking we were going to dive straight in, I squeaked, but instead he brought us down smoothly and we floated over to a dock.

I breathed a huge sigh of relief when the engines stopped, and someone tied us off. Jim hopped out of his door and disappeared. Since the dock was on my side, I wondered where he'd gone. I jumped when he appeared from nowhere to help me out. 'Th-thanks!' I stammered, happy to be on land again, albeit a jetty. Jim pulled Fluffy out too and stacked up my luggage.

There was a group of people at the end of the dock, lit by a bunch of gas torches. It was bright enough for me to see a woman with brunette hair waving enthusiastically and beaming in welcome. I looked behind me, but no one was there – she was definitely waving at me or Jim. I gave a cautious smile, carefully keeping my fangs hidden. I had no idea about vampire etiquette, but fangs felt like a threat. I thought I'd best keep them incognito until I'd made some friends, or I'd learnt how to retract them on command.

'It's your welcoming committee,' Jim explained. 'Visitors and new residents are rare. They're excited.'

'Excited about me?' I asked in disbelief. There was nothing exciting about me.

'Yeah, we don't get many Brits gracing our village. Let me be the first to welcome you.'

'Oh well, thanks! Thanks for bringing us safely here.'

'No problem.' Jim winked and helped me roll my luggage along the wooden planks. At the end, a huge burly man with long reddish-blonde hair, a prodigious beard and bright-blue eyes greeted me. 'Bunny?'

'Y-yes.'

He held out his hand. 'I'm Gunnar.' He jerked a thumb at a willowy woman with dusky skin and masses of silky dark hair, the one who had been waving at me. 'This is Sidnee. She wanted to be here to greet you.'

Sidnee grinned at me. 'Hi, Bunny. I'm so excited to meet you.'

Gunnar picked up my bags and shouldered them with ease. I wondered what kind of supernatural he was. A strong one, for sure.

'Welcome to Portlock,' he murmured. 'Your new home. You're safe here.' He placed the bags in the back of a truck.

God, I hoped so. I was thousands of miles from London, from my parents, and whoever had engineered my death. This was a new start for me in more ways than one. My escape was complete – but the case of who had ordered my dastardly death had only just begun...

The End.

Join Bunny on her next adventure in The Vampire and the Case of the Wayward Werewolf, *available to pre-order now – coming March 2024!*

Coming Soon

We hope you've enjoyed Bunny's prequel novella. Next up is *The Vampire and the Case of the Wayward Werewolf*, coming 1st March 2024! Bunny is just starting to find her feet in Alaska when there's a grisly murder...

If you'd like FREE BOOKS then join Heather's newsletter and you can get a couple of free stories, as well as pictures of her dog and other helpful things.

Jill will also give you FREE books, but she will send you cat images instead! Sign up to Jill's Newsletter for just the right amount of cat pictures.

Other Works by Heather

The *Portlock Paranormal Detective* Series with Jilleen Dolbeare

Book .5 The Vampire and the case of her Dastardly Death,

Book 1 The Vampire and the case of the Wayward Werewolf,(coming March 2024)

The *Other Realm* series

Book .5 Glimmer of Dragons (a prequel story),

Book 1 Glimmer of The Other,

Book 2 Glimmer of Hope,

Book 2.5 Glimmer of Christmas (a Christmas tale),

Book 3 Glimmer of Death,

Book 4 Glimmer of Deception,

Book 5 Challenge of the Court,

Book 6 Betrayal of the Court; and

Book 7 Revival of the Court.

The *Other Wolf* Series

Book .5 Defender of The Pack(a prequel story),

Book 1 Protection of the Pack,

Book 2 Guardians of the Pack; and

Book 3 Saviour of The Pack.

The *Other Witch* Series

Book .5 Rune of the Witch(a prequel story),

Book 1 Hex of the Witch,

Book 2 Coven of the Witch;,

Book 3 Familiar of the Witch, and

Book 4 Destiny of the Witch.

Other Works by Jilleen

The *Paranormal Portlock Detective* Series with Heather G Harris

The Vampire and the Case of Her Dastardly Death Book .5 (a prequel story), and

The Vampire and the Case of the Wayward Werewolf: Book 1 (coming March 2024).

The *Splintered Magic* Series:

Splintercat: Book .5 (a prequel story),

Splintered Magic: Book 1,

Splintered Veil: Book 2,

Splintered Fate: Book 3,

Splintered Haven: Book 4,

Splintered Secret: Book 5, and

Splintered Destiny: Book 6 (coming soon).

The *Shadow Winged* Chronicles:

Shadow Lair: Book .5 (a prequel story),

Shadow Winged: Book 1,

Shadow Wolf: Book 1.5,

Shadow Strife: Book 2 ,

Shadow Witch: Book 2.5, and

Shadow War: Book 3.

About the
Author -
Heather

About Heather

Heather is an urban fantasy writer and mum. She was born and raised near Windsor, which gave her the misguided impression that she was close to royalty in some way. She is not, though she once got a letter from Queen Elizabeth II's lady-in-waiting.

Heather went to university in Liverpool, where she took up skydiving and met her future husband. When she's not running around after her children, she's plotting her next book and daydreaming about vampires, dragons and kick-ass heroines.

Heather is a book lover who grew up reading Brian Jacques and Anne McCaffrey. She loves to travel and once spent a month in Thailand. She vows to return.

Want to learn more about Heather? Subscribe to her newsletter for behind-the-scenes scoops, free bonus material and a cheeky peek into her world. Her subscribers will always get the heads up about the best deals on her books.

Subscribe to her Newsletter at her website www.heathergharris.com/subscribe.

Too impatient to wait for Heather's next book? Join her (ever growing!) army of supportive patrons over at Patreon.

Heather's Patreon

Heather has started her very own Patreon page. What is Patreon? It's a subscription service that allows you to support Heather AND read her books way before anyone else! For a small monthly fee you could be reading Heather's next book, on a weekly chapter-by-chapter basis (in its roughest draft form!) in the next week or two. If you hit "Join the community" you can follow Heather along for FREE, though you won't get access to all the good stuff, like early release books, polls, live Q&A's, character art and more! You can even have a video call with Heather or have a character named after you! Heather's current patrons are getting to read a novella called House Bound which isn't available anywhere else, not even to her newsletter subscribers!

If you're too impatient to wait until Heather's next release, then Patreon is made for you!

Stay in Touch

Heather has been working hard on a bunch of cool things, including a new and shiny website which you'll love. Check it out at www.heathergharris.com.

If you want to hear about all Heather's latest releases – subscribe to her newsletter for news, fun and freebies. Subscribe at Heather's website www.heathergharris.com/subscribe.

Contact Info: www.heathergharris.com

Email: HeatherGHarrisAuthor@gmail.com

Social Media

Heather can also be found on a host of social medias including Facebook, Goodreads, Bookbub, and Instagram.

Reviews

Reviews feed Heather's soul. She'd really appreciate it if you could take a few moments to review her books on Amazon, Bookbub, or Goodreads and say hello.

About the
Author -
Jilleen

About Jilleen

Jilleen Dolbeare is the author of the Shadow Winged Chronicles, an urban fantasy series about a shape-shifting bush pilot in Alaska; the Splintered Magic Series, about a woman rebuilding her life and learning about magic with the help of her cat; and the Portlock Paranormal Detective Series (with Heather G. Harris) about a woman leaving her home in London, and moving to Alaska to be a detective in a small paranormal community with the help of her trusty dog.

Jilleen is the crazy cat lady in her town, walking her cats in their stroller even when that means she gets chased by wolves. She does keep her stakes sharp for those vamps that show up during the 67 days of night.

Jilleen lives with her husband and two hungry cats in Alaska where she also discovered her love and admiration of the native Alaskan people and their folklore.

Stay in Touch

Jilleen can be reached through her website https://jilleendolbeareauthor.com/

Jilleen has also just joined Patreon! What is Patreon? It's a subscription service that allows you to support Jilleen AND read her books way before anyone else! For a small monthly fee you could be reading Jill's next book, on a weekly chapter-by-chapter basis (in its roughest draft form!) in the next week or two.

If you're too impatient to wait until Jilleen's next release, then Patreon is made for you!

Social Media

Jilleen can be found on a host of social media sites so track her down on Facebook, Bookbub, Goodreads and Instagram.

Review
Request!

Wow! You finished the book. Go you!

Thanks for reading it. We appreciate it! Please, please, please consider leaving an honest review. Love it or hate it, authors can only sell books if they get reviews. If we don't sell books, Jilleen can't afford cat food. If Jilleen can't buy cat food, the little bastards will scavenge her sad, broken body. Then there will be no more books. Look at this terrifying, savage face. Jilleen's kitties have sunken cheeks and swollen tummies and can't wait to eat Jilleen. Please help by leaving that review! (Heather has a dog, so she probably won't be eaten, but she'd really like Jilleen to live, so... please review).

If you're a reviewer, you have our eternal gratitude and a gold star.

Made in United States
Orlando, FL
20 November 2023

39232603R00096